ALICE'S ADVENTURES

UNDER WATER

ALICE'S ADVENTURES

UNDER WATER

BY

LENNY DE ROOY

WITH FORTY-TWO ILLUSTRATIONS

BY ROBERT LOUIS BLACK

Nijmegen
MILLENNYUM PUBLICATIONS
2022

Alice's Adventures under Water

Published by Millennyum Publications, Nijmegen, the Netherlands
www.alice-in-wonderland.net

Written by Lenny de Rooy
Illustrated by Robert Louis Black
Printed by IngramSpark

First edition, third issue, November 2022
ISBN: 9789090346151

Copyright © 2021-2022; all rights reserved.

PREFACE

THE books *Alice's Adventures in Wonderland* and *Through the Looking-Glass and What Alice Found There* by Lewis Carroll have always been a source of inspiration for artists and writers. The book that now lies before you is therefore certainly not the first attempt to create another sequel in the series. But I have been considering writing my own version for years and I finally felt it was time to give it a try.

I've been interested in the *Alice* stories ever since I watched Disney's cartoon movie as a child. As a teenager I started researching the books and found that there is so much more to the stories than first meets the eye. I found it extremely interesting to dive into the author's background and discover in his writings so many more or less obscure references to people he knew, his personal interests, well-known poetry of the time, politics, and other elements that were prominent in the Victorian era.

Some 23 years ago, I started bundling all my findings on a website: Alice-in-wonderland.net. Nowadays many people consider me to be an expert on the stories. From this point of view, I must admit that I was often a bit disappointed in new sequels, as I always felt *something* was missing. Either the writing style did not feel very Carrollian, or the story contained little to no poetry, or the puns and jokes were not up to standard, or there were no hidden references. It may be arrogant, but I thought that, even though English is not my native language, with all my background knowledge I surely could do better?

Now I am the first to admit that I am not the greatest plot writer. Crafting a plot with many layers and character development is not my thing. However, when you look at the *Alice* stories, they don't really have much of that—it's Alice entering a dreamworld, walking from scene to scene in which she meets silly characters, and then wakes up. The story's charm lies in the wonderful, mind boggling encounters she has in a world where a completely different type of logic rules than we are used to. So I feel that a writer of an *Alice* story should primarily be able to think up silly situations, invent clever jokes, and write poetry—which is something I do feel confident about!

Besides the above, you'll find references to well known poems and songs, people, politics, and mathematics in my book. I also tried to incorporate into my story other specific elements that one can find in Carroll's *Alice* stories, like his particular use of punctuation, exactly 12 chapters, the covert return of the Hatter and the March Hare, and more. And I'm thrilled to have found the extremely talented Robert Louis Black, who accepted the challenging task of drawing 42 illustrations in the style of John Tenniel, and incorporating my crazy ideas into them! I'm also indebted to my proofreader, Michael Everson, for correcting my English grammar and spelling, and much more, so the text has achieved a quality that Carroll would have approved.

There were some concessions that had to be done, however, especially regarding the matter of dating the book. On one hand, I wanted it to have a slight antiquated feel, referring to the Victorian age in which the original *Alice* stories were written. But on the other hand, I wanted my readers to be able to recognise the references and parodies, so they can enjoy the story the same way Victorian readers were able to enjoy Carroll's works. Including modern elements would also provide me with more material to work with. After all, I did not live in Victorian times, so limiting myself to the use of people, events and works of that era would make writing a new story rather hard. Therefore I went for a more modern background, and left unspecified the year the story takes place in.

I leave it up to you as the reader to judge whether I have still succeeded in creating a story that is faithful to Lewis Carroll's originals. I can only hope that this story will delight you as much as Carroll's tales have. And perhaps you will even have as much fun with trying to find the many hidden references I put into my tale, as I had with discovering them in the original books!

Lenny de Rooy
Author and webmaster of Alice-in-wonderland.net

CONTENTS

BATTLESHIP POSITIONS

ALICE'S FLEET

Rowing boat

QUEEN BEE'S FLEET

Patrol boat

Scuttleflot

Alice to arrive in her rowing boat, and win in seven turns.

Long ago there was a boat
    With sisters on a river.
They asked a tale while being afloat
    Which Dodgson did deliver.
It was a feat, and so he wrote
    A manuscript to give her.

Surely he had no idea
    His stories would entail
Such impact on their reader's glee,
    And spread on global scale.
World-famous fairy-tales they'd be
    For ages to prevail.

His stories with their curious creatures
    Are to us all familiar:
Humpty Dumpty trying to teach us,
    The Jabberwock and its killer,
And also Chapter Five that features
    A smoking Caterpillar!

Many volumes have been sold
    Of Dodgson's works of art.
So often have the tales been told
    That pages fall apart—
But still they bring me joy and hold
    A place within my heart.

I therefore feel they qualify
    For further continuation.
Before you lies the proof that I
    Could not resist temptation.
I hope you'll be delighted by
    My very own creation!

CHAPTER I

Taking the Plunge

ALICE stumbled out of the rowing boat, slightly relieved to be back on land. It had been all nice and fun to float on the little waves the wind had created in the water, to take turns in rowing, and to "accidentally" splash water on her sisters, but by now the sun was getting *very* hot on her head, which made her sweaty and uncomfortable. One of her sisters had remarked that she could see her face getting red, "and that is not a good thing at all," she thought, "for if people can read my face, I will never be able to keep a secret again! 'Alice,' they will ask, 'did you or did you not take a snack from the jar without permission?' And then they will be able to read the answer from my face, as it will resemble the pages of that dull book I have to finish for my literature lessons."

Pondering about how she could make herself look innocent again without having to resort to peeling her skin off (which would, very likely, only make the redness worse), Alice wandered off from the rest of the party. A little further at the shore of the lake she noticed a small rock formation. She knelt down on it and leaned slightly forward in an attempt to see her own reflection in the water, so she would be able to determine exactly what state her face currently was in.

By now there was no more wind, which meant the sun felt even hotter, but also that the smooth surface of the water remained intact. Slowly, Alice began to see her face appear, mirrored in the wet surface. Immediately her mind began to wander off again, as it often did (especially during lessons, for which she was always scolded by her tutor, who unfortunately could *not* understand that a tiny spider building its little web is oh! so more interesting than a grammar lesson).

"I wonder if it is actually me whom I see in the water?" Alice asked herself. "How do I know it is not *another* Alice, living down there in the lake, who is looking back at me?"

Alice peered deeper into the water. If she focused her eyes a bit differently, she could see both her own reflection and that of her surroundings, as well as dirt and other objects that floated beneath the surface.

"It looks as if there are two worlds *together* down there!" she observed. "A bit of our world, and a bit of the under-water world."

Alice tilted a little more forward. What *was* that dark lump over there, just behind that leaf?

All of a sudden, a large red herring shot past, splashing up droplets of water when its back cut through the surface.

"Oh!" cried Alice, very much startled, and hastily scrambled back from the edge. But alas, the sudden movement caused her to lose her balance. Her foot slipped on the wet rock and *splash!* in she went!

The water was not as cold as she thought it would be. In fact, it felt rather pleasant to her skin. Alice noticed how her clothes began sucking up water and how her dress went upwards and started fluttering all around her— (like a ballet dancer making a pirouette,

she thought—only she was moving downwards instead of turning around on her axis), — and how she felt herself become heavier and heavier each second. Not only did she feel as if she were becoming heavier, she also felt that she was becoming *smaller.* "But that must be all in my mind," she thought: "of course it looks like things down there are getting larger. After all, I keep getting closer to them!" And she was rather pleased with her ability to assess her situation so well.

But as the journey down took quite a long time, Alice began to worry. "How *will* I be able to breathe down here?" she asked herself. "I will have to start doing that again sometime soon, seeing how far down I have sunk into this lake already! It is so much deeper than I thought it would be!" Her mother had always warned her to stay away from deep waters, in case she would fall in and drown. However, she considered that it was a little late to adhere to that advice now. There was no way to reverse her sinking. Or was there?

"What if I were to blow out air towards the bottom?" she thought. "Would it perhaps propel me upwards, back to the shore?" It seemed like a very clever idea, so she decided to try it. Indeed, large bubbles of air shot out of her mouth and started floating upwards. But poor Alice just kept sinking further.

"Now what do I do?" Alice asked herself. Then she remembered her history lessons. "Perhaps I could try to grow a pair of gills instead of lungs. According to Mr Darwin this should be possible, if I only wait long enough—or is it the other way around? And how long exactly would it take?" Alice touched her neck and cheeks to check whether or not she could already feel anything growing there, but to her disappointment everything felt completely ordinary. "It should not take much longer than this," she thought impatiently, "as I am sure I shall not be able to hold my breath much longer!"

Suddenly Alice reached the bottom of the lake. She had not seen it coming, being so busy trying to work out how to handle the situation, and it startled her so much that she gave a little shriek. That is—it would have sounded like a shriek under normal circumstances, but opening her mouth now only made water get in instead of sound come out. To Alice's surprise, this was no problem at all. She was able to breathe the water as easily as she had been able to breathe air. "Well, that *is* a relief," Alice thought.

After having inhaled and exhaled several times, just to be sure that she wasn't drowning, Alice curiously looked up to the surface. She saw no reflection of herself peering down the lake. "Does that mean I have now become under-water Alice?" she wondered. "Or perhaps above-water Alice and under-water Alice have merged into one, just as I saw in the reflection? Being two people at the same time *would* explain why I am feeling so much heavier now."

"Perhaps that means that I now also know twice as many things as I used to!" she speculated enthusiastically. "Oh, how nice it would be to be able to skip half of my lessons! Well, let's put it to the test: I'll try and repeat a little poem." And so Alice stood upright and began:—

"That is in fact right," Alice giggled, rather amused, "although it is not exactly how *I* learned it. I seem to know more than one version of the poem now. That proves it! I most certainly have become two people in one! But what will happen if I want to get out of the water again? Will the two of me be able to nicely split ourselves up again? Or is there a risk that under-water Alice will keep remembering all the things above-water Alice has studied so hard on, and that above-water Alice's mind will go completely blank? That would *not* be something to look forward to, as it would mean having to learn all my lessons all over again!" Alice worried. After reflecting on that scenario a little, she continued: "Or, perhaps I might have to choose which body parts are allowed to leave the water. I would probably choose my head. But then, how will I be able to reach home without my feet?" Ah, this *was* a puzzle for Alice!

Another thought struck her: how quickly would she age down here? After all, when she took long baths, her skin would go all wrinkly. "I will have to mind that one grows older much more quickly while being submerged in water, since Time runs faster in water than in air," she thought. She now began to understand why her mother always scolded her for keeping the tap running unnecessarily. "If Time already runs fast in stagnant water, like the water in my tub," Alice considered, "how fast he will have to run to keep up if the water itself is running as well! Poor Time, it must be exhausting!" Alice now regretted ignoring her mother's directions, and forcing Time to run unnecessarily because of her carelessness. She decided to pay better attention to closing the tap, once she was back home.

"But how am I to handle Time down here?" Alice wondered. She imagined herself emerging from the lake as some kind of ancient, shrivelled monster. "Nobody will recognise me and I will have to introduce myself all over again to everybody. 'Excuse me, sir—I'm Alice, your daughter'—no, that just wouldn't do! But then," Alice continued, "my skin always goes back to normal quite soon after I get out of the bath. That probably means that my aging will get reversed once I get out of the lake as well. Yes, that must be the case! So perhaps if I am careful not to stay for too long, and accidentally die down here before I have had a chance to return, I could see just a little more of this strange place. Because it *would* be a pity not having a chance to explore it, now that I'm here!"

This started yet another train of thought. Would the inhabitants here have clocks, so she would be able to track time? "They could have, as clocks run on current, and they have that down here as well. Except, it is water current. So the clocks here must be running on WC instead of AC and DC," she concluded—although she did not like to admit to herself that she did not exactly know what that meant or if it made any sense at all. But as there was nobody else here to hear her, let alone correct her, it did not matter.

While she was thinking about how to properly proceed her stay under water, the red herring shot past her again, breaking her chain of thought. It looked much larger than it had been when she first saw it jump out of the water. In fact, it was now almost as large as she was! "Or," thought Alice: "am I now as *small* as *it* is?"

Either way, Alice realised that she could not remain seated on the lake bottom forever—if she wouldn't be able to stay for long, she needed to hurry if she would want to get a peek at everything down here. "Which must surely be very interesting!" she thought. But where to go first? Alice looked in the direction where the red herring had disappeared and noticed little bubbles of air rising up from behind a rock. Curiously, Alice got up and decided to take a look.

CHAPTER II

The Game Begins

WHEN she reached the rock and took a peep behind it, Alice discovered a fish wallowing itself in the bubbles of air, which appeared to come out of a hole in the ground. It was a funny sight, but Alice thought it was somewhat improper to observe the fish like this, as it felt as if she was invading its privacy. But right when she was about to walk away, it noticed her. Alice feared that walking away now would probably be just as rude, if not even ruder. Not knowing how to handle the situation, she just blurted out an introduction.

"Hello, my name is Alice. What is yours?"

"My name is Irrelevant," replied the Fish.

Alice was taken aback. She had not expected the Fish to *actually reply*, let alone so impolitely. Although she had to admit that her knowledge of etiquette regarding the addressing of fish was quite limited, this response felt rather ill-mannered regardless. So she replied: "I'm not sure this is the appropriate way to start—"

"On the contrary," said the Fish, "I start every afternoon like this. Freshens me up and keeps me going. Speaking of which: did you wash your brain properly this morning?"

"I beg your pardon?" said Alice, confused by the apparent change of topic.

"You didn't?" said the Fish. "You shouldn't think with a dirty mind! It's unhygienic."

"But how am I supposed to wash my brain?" Alice protested.

"The same way you wash your hands before having breakfast, lunch, or dinner, of course. Don't you do that either?"

Before Alice could respond, the Fish continued: "How about your teeth? Have you combed your teeth this morning?"

"Combed? You mean brushed?" corrected Alice.

"No, combed," said the Fish. "You use a brush for your hair, silly!"

"Yes, that's true," Alice admitted. "But you can use a brush for your teeth as well. A comb is for your hair only."

"Are you mad?" said the Fish. "Tell me, what is on a brush?"

Alice considered. "Well—hair, I suppose. Mine is made of pig hair."

"Exactly," said the Fish. "And what is on a comb?"

Alice hesitated. "Uhm—teeth?"

"There you go," said the Fish. "So you should use a brush for your hair and a comb for your teeth, eh, stupid?"

Alice didn't like being criticised about her grooming habits like this at all. "Why are you so crabby?" she said indignantly.

"Crabby?" said the Fish. "Not at all; I'm just a little Peefish."

Alice thought it looked nothing like it, but wisely decided to try to steer the conversation to a more neutral subject. "May I ask what you are doing?" she asked instead.

"I'm washing myself," exclaimed the Fish, "if that was not obvious already!"

"Washing?" asked Alice in a surprised voice. "In air?"

"Yes, of course," the Fish said impatiently. "You humans wash yourself with water and walk through air. So wouldn't it make sense that down here, where we swim through water, we wash ourselves with air? It's the same with breathing and drinking. You drink water and breathe in air, we drink air and breathe in water. As both are done with mouths, you are fully capable of living under water as well—as long as you are prepared to adapt to our culture."

"And how about using my nose?" asked Alice. "Can one smell down here?"

"Yes, one can," replied the Fish, "but it will keep you awake. So don't do it in the evening or you wo'n't get any sleep."

Alice did not understand why, but decided not to press the matter, as the Fish already appeared to be very annoyed with her questions.

All of a sudden, there was a loud splash about thirty feet to their right—as if a large object from above had just hit the water.

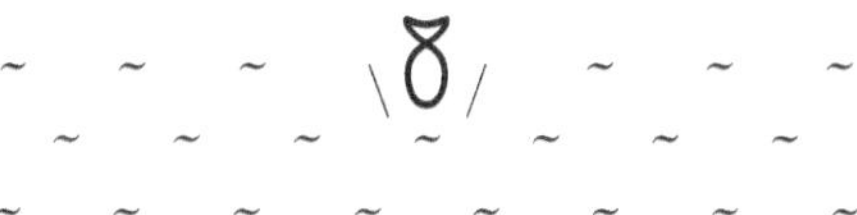

Alice froze. "What was that?" she cried.

"That was the Scuttleflot," said the Fish. "The Queen Bee just had it drop a bombshell."

Alice was both bewildered and alarmed. "What is a Scuttleflot? Who is the Queen Bee? And *why* is she dropping bombs?" she exclaimed.

"Did you arrive here by boat?" the Fish inquired.

"Well, we were rowing on top of the lake with a boat. But my arrival here was more or less by plunge, after we docked," admitted Alice.

"That explains it," said the Fish. "The Queen Bee has noticed the presence of your rowing boat and she considers it a threat to her empire."

"You mean she wants to sink our rowing boat?" Alice cried out. "She ca'n't do that!"

"Well, we'll have to see if she can. But she just proved that she is at least capable of attempting it," said the Fish.

This did not reassure Alice at all. "What if she actually hits it? We will have to walk all the way back home!"

The Fish shrugged. (That is, Alice thought it did—it was rather hard to see where its shoulders started and where they ended.) "You could swim. Nothing wrong with that."

Alice did not look forward to having to explain to the others what had happened to their boat and how they now should *all* get wet in order to get home in time before dark. "We did not mean to intrude. And we are no threat to the Queen at all!" pleaded Alice.

"That may very well be," said the Fish, "but *she* does not know that."

"Then I must go to her and explain!" decided Alice.

"Too late," said the Fish. "The game has already started."

"Game?" said Alice. "This is no game! I don't want to participate in any of this!"

"You have no choice," said the Fish.

"But—" Alice protested.

"It's your turn now, by the way."

"What? I'd first like to be—" Alice started saying.

"2B it is!" the Fish shouted, interrupting her.

And before Alice could say anything else, a large shell that had been hidden under the sand next to her was propelling upwards with great speed. It

24

penetrated the water line and immediately got out of sight. A few seconds later she heard a muffled crash, not far away.

"You hit her patrol boat!" cheered the Fish. "Well done!"

"But—" Alice tried protesting again.

"You're good at this!" said the Fish. "Do continue. You now know how it works, so I'll just leave you to it." And it started packing up its things.

Alice was getting quite frustrated. "As I said, I have no intention to play any game! I mean the Queen and her empire no harm, and I need her to stop bombarding our boat as soon as possible! Please, would you tell me where I might find her, so I can explain the situation?"

The Fish had finished packing its belongings and began to swim off.

"Where can I find the Queen Bee?" Alice asked it again.

"It goes without saying," replied the Fish, and to Alice's frustration it did indeed.

As there was no one else left to ask for directions, Alice decided to continue walking in the direction where she had seen the red herring disappear. Not after long, she came upon a house that had obviously been submerged for quite some time. It was almost completely covered with seaweed and shells. Little sea creatures were swimming through the open windows. In front of the house there was a goldfish, swimming amidst high stacks of books, intently comparing the content of two of them.

"Good day," Alice said, this time avoiding any introductions. "Can you please tell me why there is a house at the bottom of this lake?"

The Goldfish looked up from its books. "I'm sorry, I'm afraid I cannot. That would be inappropriate. History repeats itself, you know."

Before Alice could figure out what it meant by that, all of a sudden a majestic and solemn voice came out of nowhere:—

"Once upon a midnight creepy, while I pondered, tired and sleepy,
Over many a dull and tedious recurrence of orbiculate stroll—
While I floated, there was consilience, and suddenly a stroke of
    brilliance,
Creating strong resilience, happening in my goldfish bowl.
'Tis a turnaround,' I fluttered, 'happening in my goldfish bowl—
        There's more than this, this swimming hole!'

Ah, distinctly I concluded that this water was polluted,
And each separate day I swam here did just break my heart and
    soul.
Eagerly I wished escaping;—vainly I had tried landscaping,
But no single act of draping had improved my goldfish bowl—
For there was no way to liven up my tiny goldfish bowl—
        Forever dull this wretched hole.

26

Then the emanating glee in my short-term memory
Thrilled me—filled me with excitement never matched by a sausage
    roll;
So that now, to take some action, swam I with a drill contraption
Towards the glass refraction and at once I took control—
I reached the glass refraction and once there I took control;
                        Poked and cracked to bore a hole.

But because the glass's thickness, adding to its very slickness,
Soon I came to the conclusion that I would not reach my goal.
This darn bowl wo'n't take disjointing, which is surely
    disappointing;
I can see a prospect daunting: to be jailed without parole—
I'll forever be unhappy when I'm jailed without parole;—
                        So unable to drill a hole.

'Open now!' I shouted loudly, while my tears rolled down
    unproudly,
I had no idea my crying would be taking such a toll.
Only recognising slowly, that the waters rose below me,
And I made it overflow, see! Filling up my goldfish bowl—
Saw the water level rising just above my goldfish bowl—
                        Escaped, and swam, without a hole!

And the water, never slowing, still kept flowing, still kept flowing
From the house into the gardens all around my goldfish bowl;
Still this water kept on streaming and it muffled all my screaming
Any chance of stopping seeming far beyond my own control.
So the waters kept expanding far beyond my own control,
                        And engulfed—every soul!"

"Oh," exclaimed Alice, "so that is why the water is so salty here!"

"Yes," said the Goldfish. "And it made me King of this lake. Sadly, the Queen Bee took over some time ago. Now all I own is this piece of land around the house."

"Can you tell me why there is a Queen Bee? What is a bee even doing in a lake?" inquired Alice.

"You'd better ask my gardener," said the Goldfish. "He's even more fond of explaining things than I am. You can find him at the back of the house."

Alice thanked the Goldfish and walked around the house. There she discovered a pretty little garden, although it was full of weeds. The Gardener was busy scribbling things on little wooden signs and sticking them in front of the plants. He looked up from his work when he heard Alice coming.

"Hello, can I help you?" he asked.

"Yes, please, if you would," Alice replied. "Your employer told me to ask you why your Queen is a bee, and how come she is living in a lake."

"I will tell you, with pleasure," said the Gardener, leaning on his rake. "Actually, she used to be a flying fish. When she tried taking over power in this lake, my boss had her beeheaded. But it did not make much of a difference, unfortunately. She's a rather unpleasant beeing, that I can tell you!"

Alice thought that it was probable that any one would get unpleasant and nasty if they were beheaded. Regardless, it had not been nice of her to try to take away the Goldfish's land. "How do you feel about her having taken over?" Alice asked the Gardener.

"I don't like it one bit, of course! So I'm very grateful that I can keep working this land here, as that still belongs to my boss. He will never give it up. Nor will my boss sell one good acre to that Queen!" the Gardener exclaimed, while shaking his fin to nobody in particular.

"I hope you'll be able to keep it forever," said Alice. "Are you not afraid that she'll bomb you? She's trying to sink our rowing boat, you know!"

"Ah yes, that's what she does. But we don't own a boat, so we're quite safe against the Scuttleflot," said the Gardener.

"What is this Scuttleflot I keep hearing about?" asked Alice.

"Nobody knows for sure. It is said that it is a very dangerous creature, half monster, half boat," the Gardener explained.

"Half monster and half boat?" Alice exclaimed with incredulity. "How can that be?"

"The story goes," said the Gardener, "that it once tried to eat a boat. But in its greed it tried to swallow it whole. Then the boat got stuck in its belly and wouldn't digest. And as it also engulfed all the air that was in it, it couldn't get to the bottom of the lake anymore. It is said that over time the boat and the creature just kind of merged into one another."

"Doesn't swallowing all that air also cause a very bad case of gas?" Alice ventured to ask.

"Yes," said the Gardener. "That is what causes the currents in the lake. Eventually all the air will leave the Scuttleflot, and then it will be able to come down again. But let's hope that wo'n't happen anytime soon!"

Alice tried to imagine what a half-boat, half-monster creature would look like, but found it quite impossible to wrap her mind around the idea. The only thing she did know, is that she did not want to meet it. And that she *certainly* wasn't going to confront it because of its attempt at sinking their boat. No, she would much rather face the Queen Bee instead, she decided.

"I don't think it's fair at all," said Alice in a sulky tone. We didn't know that we weren't supposed to be on this lake with our boat. And the Queen Bee gave me no chance to explain either! She just instructed the Scuttleflot to bombard it when she noticed it."

"That is her way," said the Gardener, his reply being somewhat drowned out by the sound of something heavy hitting the water a bit farther off.

"Apparently she has a tendency to overreact," muttered Alice.

For the second time, a shell sped upwards from the sand next to her, startling her once again.

"Ah, I see you've already learned how to play," said the Gardener, nodding approvingly. "But you can only make one move per turn, you know. The first one counts."

"I don't want to play! And I don't know why this happens!" complained Alice. "I only want to speak to the Queen Bee and tell her this is all one big misunderstanding!"

“Well, good luck with that,” said the Gardener, shaking his head. “I don’t think you’ll have much chance. She’s always buzzy.”

“I need to try. Please, can you tell me where to find her?” Alice asked.

The Gardener sighed and pointed towards the back of the garden. “Go that way. You’ll need to cross some meadows first.”

“Thank you very much,” said Alice, and started off in the direction the Gardener had pointed out to her.

CHAPTER III

Permits and Passings

THERE were indeed several patches of rather plain meadows behind the garden, not at all as lovely as the garden had been. In the middle of the first meadow a horse stood grazing weeds.

"Hello, Mr Horse!" Alice shouted to it cheerfully when she passed.

"That's Mr *Seahorse*," answered the Seahorse, hardly looking up from its lunch.

"I beg your pardon," said Alice. "It's just that you don't look like a seahorse. And also, this is a lake and not a sea, is it not?"

"What do I look like to you, then?" asked the Seahorse.

"You look like a horse," said Alice. "And there is nothing wrong with that, of course!" she added quickly, to avoid offending the animal. "They're very noble animals, you know."

"Exactly so," said the Seahorse. "So you're saying that if you look at me, you *see a horse*. Yet you call me something else. Do you always call things differently than what they look like to you? Do you call people out? Do you call forth a spirit? Do you call exes wise? Well?"

"Well, I suppose I sometimes do," confessed Alice, thinking about how she sometimes confronted her sister when she had been playing with her toys again without asking.

"Hmpf," growled the Seahorse. "Then what should *I* call *you*?"

"Alice—or human, depending on what you are referring to," said Alice. "The first is my name, the second my species. Or is it my genus?" Alice desperately tried to recall her biology lessons.

"It gets confusing quickly, eh?" said the Seahorse. "I'll just stick to naming things the way they appear to me. I think I will call you Miss Leading."

Alice was not at all pleased with that name, but did not feel like starting an argument. A thought came to her. Even though it called itself a seahorse, it did have the shape of a land horse.

"Well, Sir, I would like to meet the Queen Bee. Could you please take me to her on your back?" she asked politely.

The Seahorse sighed. "If fishes were horses, beggars would ride!" it said, and yawned.

"I'm sorry," excused Alice, trying to hide her disappointment. "You seem to be tired. I'll just walk then."

"Tired?" said the Seahorse in an offended tone, "I'm not tired! I already told you I am a seahorse! I'm not a horse, and nor am I a cart! I have legs to walk with, just as you have!"

As it was obvious that the Seahorse insisted on taking everything she said the wrong way, Alice thought the best thing to do was to leave it alone. It hardly paid any attention to her anyway when she said good-bye—it had already busied itself again with chewing weeds.

Alice continued her walk through the meadows, wondering how far she would have to walk before she would be able to meet with the Queen Bee. And if she would be allowed to meet her at all—she had not even considered yet how a common girl like herself would be able to acquire an invitation to meet royalty!

As soon as Alice had reached the far end of the very last meadow, she came upon a wooden fence with a gate. Several creatures were perched on the fence surrounding the gate—one of them was holding a nasty looking pike. And they were all looking at Alice.

They reminded Alice so much of a poem, that she couldn't help repeating it aloud. Only it was under-water Alice's version that emerged from her mouth:—

> *"Five little fishes, sitting on a gate;*
> *The first one said, "We should be losing weight."*
> *The second one said, "This gate's about to break!"*
> *The third one said, "I want a piece of cake."*
> *The fourth one said, "Let's eat, and eat, and eat."*
> *The fifth one said, "I'm ready for a treat!"*
> *Then cra—a—a—ash went the gate, and DOWN went they all,*
> *And five little fishes thus lay asprawl!"*

"Fishes? I'm not a fish!" the first creature said crabbily.

"And I'm not overweight!" grunted the fourth.

"Actually, I wouldn't mind a bit of food—" said the fifth creature.

"Of course you wouldn't!" snapped the third. "You'd likely be so selfish as to bring us all down!"

"I wouldn't!" said the Shellfish. "I'm just hungry! Why, I haven't left this fence in ages. They never send any replacements here, never!"

At that point, all the creatures began mumbling and muttering to themselves, about how it was very unfair indeed that they were being stuck here and not very well taken care of.

"Who is your employer then?" asked Alice.

"It's the Queen Bee, of course," said the Grunter. "We are here to make sure that her empire is well guarded."

"Well," thought Alice, "at least I'm heading in the right direction. But I hope they'll allow me to go through that gate." She eyed the Pike, which was still looking quite nasty. And looking back at her as well. In her nicest voice, she said: "I would like to visit the Queen Bee, please. I have important matters to discuss with her. I was told to pass here."

"She needs to pass here," said the Snapper to the Crab.

“Did you study?” asked the Grunter.

“I did not m—” Alice began to say.

“She didn’t!” exclaimed the Grunter. “Then how do you expect to be able to pass?”

“The way I see it, you have two options,” the Snapper concluded. “Either turn back, or try to pass unprepared.”

Turning back did not sound like an attractive option to Alice, as she knew no other way to get to the Queen. And a detour would only increase the chances that the Scuttleflot would sink their boat before she had been able to explain the situation. So she took a deep breath and said in a nervous voice: “I would like to try right now please.”

“All right, here we go,” said the Snapper. “What do you get when you add two to four?”

“Six,” said Alice, relieved that the test apparently wouldn’t be too hard.

“Wrong!” said the Snapper. “Together they make 42.”

"She's not very bright," decided the Grunter. "Let's ask a more simple question. What colour is the inside of your eyelids?"

"I don't know—" hesitated Alice.

"How can you not know?" exclaimed the Grunter. "Why, you look at it several times a minute! What a very ignorant child you are. You should always pay attention. Then, ask for a receipt, and fill out a form to get your taxes back."

"What is the answer to the question, then?" Alice asked crossly.

"I have no idea," it answered. "How would *I* know? I'm a fish—I don't have eyelids! Another question: what would happen if a plant started shooting?"

Alice could not even begin to wrap her head around the concept of armed vegetation, and was really getting frustrated by now. "It beats me," she said in a defiant tone.

"Wrong again," the Grunter said cheerfully. "It wouldn't beat you, it wood make tree boughs, bark, and leaf." And they all giggled.

"All right, I give up!" cried Alice. "I'll never guess the answers to your silly questions!"

"Obviously you wo'n't. You're the only one who's left," said the Snapper.

"The only one who's left?" Alice asked, feeling puzzled. "Where are the others then?"

"*They* were the ones who were right, of course!" it answered. "Let's try something other than questions. Tell us a story. Tell us about what you are doing here."

"Yes," cried the Shellfish, "but do it inverse!"

This *was* a challenge for poor Alice. She sat down and thought about it for some time. But after a little while, she felt confident enough and began decisively:—

"Queen Bee had a Scuttleflot,
It looked much like a boat;
And every time it dived forgot
That it could only float.

It followed me to shore one day,
While I was unaware;
It made me join their game and play,
And gave me quite a scare.

By chance I shot at it at will,
But still it drifted near;
And waited patiently until
My shell would disappear.

The Queen called for another shot
Again it sought my craft;
As if it said 'I'll find your spot';
It launched its shell and laughed.

What makes the Queen dislike me so,
Why does she cause me pain?
'Oh, I'm just passing by, you know'
I want to go explain.

Then I can only hope she'll see
That I want this to end;
Once they stop throwing shells at me
I shall get back to land."

"There," thought Alice, very proud of herself for having come up with this in such a short time, "I'm sure I did this one right! They *must* let me pass now!" But while she stood looking proudly about her, the Grunter shouted: "Wrong *again!*"

"It's *not* wrong!" said Alice indignantly. "This story is very much true. If any one can be the judge of that, it's me! And I even made it rhyme, as you requested!"

"We did no such thing," said the Snapper. "We asked you to do the opposite."

"Indeed," said the Crab, "you should have told us something about what you don't do at home."

"I don't mind questions or assignments," said Alice scornfully, feeling she was beginning to lose her temper, "but you should be more clear about the rules! This is completely unfair!"

"I'm positive you're being too negative," said the Snapper. "We were *very* clear about them—and if you *would* have minded about the questions, you would have answered them correctly!"

With a sigh, Alice sat down on the ground, trying to suppress her tears. "How am I *ever* to get to the other side of the fence," she sighed, "when I cannot pass this test?"

"You want to get to the other side of this fence? Oh, but you don't need to pass a test for that," said the Crab.

"What?" Alice cried out furiously. "Then why did you ask me all these questions in the first place?"

"Because *you* said you needed it," replied the Shellfish. "We were just trying to help."

It took Alice several seconds to calm herself down. Then she said, as controlled as she could manage: "Never mind. Can you just open that gate now?"

"I ca'n't," said the Snapper.

"Why not?" cried Alice in great dismay. "What is it *this* time?"

"To be allowed to go through the gate, you'll need a permit," said the Crab.

"And how do I get one of those?" Alice asked, trying to contain her temper as best as she could manage, although she felt she really could not take any more of this.

"Simply wait until one swims by. And then have it officialised," the Crab said. "Look, there's one now!" And it pointed to a massive, rather flat fish, that just happened to be calmly swimming by in their vicinity. "Hurry up, and get it before it swims away!"

Alice immediately ran after it, but it was much faster than she had anticipated. Every time she got near it, it quickly took a sharp turn and swam into another direction. The faster she ran, the faster it swam. After having run across the meadow five times without even managing to touch its tail, Alice gave up. Exhausted, she returned to the five creatures on the fence. "This is impossible! I'll never be able to catch it!"

"That's where you go wrong," said the Crab. "You shouldn't try to catch it—a permit needs to be signed!"

Alice wondered about this for a moment and then decided to attempt waving at it. The Permit looked in her direction. "Well, this at least seems to do *something*," she thought. "Let's try something else." And she made a gesture with her hand, beckoning it to come closer. To her surprise, this worked like a charm! The fish swam towards her and kept floating next to her. "Now what?" Alice asked the Crab.

"Now you'll need to get it watermarked," it said.

"And how am I supposed to do *that*?" Alice asked, not wanting to put anymore effort into fruitless endeavours.

"Roll over it. Dandily," the Crab answered.

Alice wondered if they were trying to play a joke on her. Surely they could not be serious about her having to *roll over a fish*? But they all looked very serious. Alice sighed. "Very well." She looked at the Permit and pointed towards the ground. The Permit swam down. Then, she made a flipping gesture. Without hesitating, the fish turned itself over so it floated parallel to the ground, almost touching it. Alice gathered her courage and, not wanting to actually touch it (as its skin looked rather slimy and she also did not want to hurt the fish), tried her best at doing a gracious somersault over the creature, landing on the other side of the fish, and subsequently twirling and raising her arms in an attempt to make a nice show out of it, like she had seen gymnasts do at the end of their routines.

The five all clapped.

"Congratulations," said the Snapper. "You've now got yourself an official permit to go to the other side of the gate!"

"Finally," sighed Alice.

The Grunter jumped off the fence and trudged towards the gate to open it. "Good luck!" it called after her, "And don't forget to study the next time you want to take a test!"

CHAPTER IV

Pies at Present

ALICE did not look back and made sure she got far away from the gate as quickly as she could, before the creatures changed their minds and came up with yet another impossible assignment. After having walked on for some time, she came upon a rock on which a catlike creature was standing. It stood straight up on its hind paws, peering intently over the area. Then it looked at her.

"Duck!" it said.

Alice looked around, but didn't see any ducks.

"Duck!" it said once more.

For a moment Alice thought it was mistaking *her* for a duck. But then, a shell shot through the water at high speed, barely missing her head.

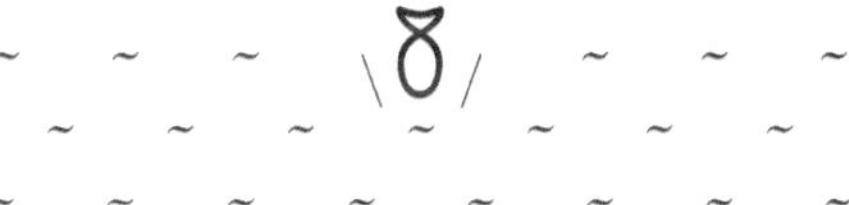

"You have very good eyes, to see that one coming," gasped Alice.

A shell rose up from beside her and propelled out of the water with the same speed the other one had entered through. This time though, she thought she could hear a small explosion further off as well.

"I wish it would stop doing that," muttered Alice.

The creature just continued to stand straight up on the rock, looking at her disapprovingly.

"Thank you for trying to warn me. Who are you, and what are you doing in this lake?" asked Alice. "Did you fall in, just like me?"

"My name is Villikins," he answered. "And I live in this lake, because I'm a meerkat."

"But you don't look like a meerkat," said Alice, quite forgetting the conversation she had had with the Seahorse. "And they don't belong in a lake either."

"Actually, they do," said the Meerkat. "But I'm used to people getting confused. I'm originally from the Netherlands, you see."

Alice did not see. "You look somewhat like my cat, Dinah," she said. "She has the same pretty long whiskers."

"Your cat, does she purr?" Villikins asked.

"Of course," replied Alice, "especially when she lies in my lap or when I pet her."

"Then why did you not bring her?" asked Villikins.

"Bring her? Why should I have?" asked Alice, who was sure Dinah wouldn't have liked the water at all.

"Because you shouldn't go anywhere without a purrpuss," the Meerkat stated. "Yet here you are, in all purrpusslessness."

"Is that even a word?" Alice wanted to ask, but before she could say it out loud, a small yet hard thing hit Alice in the back of her head. "Ouch!" she exclaimed, and turned around to see what caused it. There was no one to be seen, but a little pebble was lying on the ground behind her. She picked it up and placed it on the rock next to Villikins. "Do pebbles always fly around here?" she asked him. But instead of answering, Villikins only looked at her with an intense stare. Very, very slowly, and without losing eye contact, he shoved the pebble off the rock with one of his paws. Alice saw it roll away and disappear into a hole in the ground.

"Why did you—" she started, but before she could finish her sentence, she felt another pebble hitting her head. She quickly turned around and this time she was just in time to see the head of a second meerkat disappear into one of several holes in the ground. She turned back to Villikins. "Is that a member of your family? It is behaving rather—*ouch!*" Again she turned around. There now was a slightly different-looking meerkat peeking out of a hole a bit further off, but this one made no effort to hide. And it was holding another pebble. "Just you wait," said Alice in an aggravated tone, and walked towards the meerkat. But before she could grab the pebble out of its paws, it retracted into the hole. At the same time yet another meerkat emerged from a hole, throwing a pebble at her. Alice ran towards it, but was too late again.

The scene repeated itself for quite a while: each time Alice thought she could grab the meerkat, it disappeared right before her eyes and another one emerged somewhere else. "It's just like playing whack-a-mole!" she cried in dismay. "Or rather, whack-a-cat!" Unfortunately her remark only seemed to encourage the creatures, because now every time one popped its head out of a hole, it chittered: "Whackacat! Whackacat!" Eventually Alice's head *really* began to hurt and she decided to give up trying to catch the creatures, as they were quick as lightning. Instead, she picked up several large stones and put them on top of each opening, effectively sealing them off. "That should teach you!" she said.

Just when she had put the last stone in place, Alice's stomach began to growl. This did not surprise her at all, for she had not eaten anything since breakfast. "The others must have begun the picnic on the riverbank by now," she realised sadly. "I wonder if they'll save some food for me." She had seen the things her mother had packed into the picnic basket for them and would definitely be *very* disappointed if she would not get any of it. Her stomach growled again. Alice looked up and noticed that Villikins now stood in a crouch, his tail slowly wagging back and forth, while he was intently staring at Alice.

"What are you looking at?" asked Alice, a little worried.

Villikins did not say anything. He kept his eyes focused on Alice.

"I am merely hungry," she tried to explain.

"Hungry—indeed," Villikins said. "And you are going to eat *me*?"

"Of course not!" cried Alice. "Why would you think that?"

"Because you growled at me," said the Meerkat. "That means you might be going to attack me."

"Oh please don't worry," exclaimed Alice, trying not to laugh. "It was just my stomach growling, not me!"

"Is your stomach going to eat *me*?" asked the Meerkat, not relaxing for a bit.

"No, I don't like meerkats," said Alice. "And therefore my stomach doesn't either. I could do with some human food though. Would you happen to know where I can find some?"

The Meerkat relaxed, but kept eyeing Alice suspiciously. "Go to the house over there, they always have plenty," he said.

"Thank you," said Alice. She could distinguish an angular shape in the direction the Meerkat had pointed towards, and assumed this would be the house. When she continued, she indeed came upon a rather small building. It was perfectly square, and its walls were beautifully adorned with glossy paper. A shiny bow perched on top of the flat roof. In its garden Alice found a jellyfish, sitting with its eyes closed and all its legs crossed. "Or is it 'with all its arms crossed'?" Alice wondered. "I wouldn't know which is which!" She tiptoed towards the house, trying not to disturb the jellyfish as it looked so concentrated and peaceful. But when she got closer, it opened one eye.

"I'm sorry, I did not mean to disturb your meditation," Alice said apologetically.

"That's okay," said the Jellyfish, opening its second eye as well. "I'm no good at it at all, anyway. I suppose I'm too weak minded for it. Would you like some pie?"

"Thank you," said Alice. "That is very hospitable and generous of you!"

"Not at all," said the Jellyfish. "Pie comes in an infinite number, you see. Also, it does not make sense to divide it with none." It went inside the house and after a moment it came back with very tasty-looking pastry, which made Alice even more hungry immediately. The Jellyfish carefully cut the pie into pieces, using not only a knife but also a tape measure, hygrometer, chronometer, and thermometer. "To make sure all pieces are *exactly* the same," it explained.

Alice wondered why it mattered. "If pie comes in an infinite number, you could always take another piece if you felt you got too little of it, could you not?"

"That pie is infinitely available does not mean its amount shouldn't be fixed!" warned the Jellyfish. "It is actually very important to have a fixed amount of pie. Otherwise greedy people would be tempted to enlarge the pie—which would cause the pieces you can cut from it to become smaller!"

Alice felt dreadfully puzzled. If you made a pie larger, wouldn't it make sense that the pieces you could cut from it became larger as well? She decided she did not want to think about it, as all this talk about pie made her even more hungry. So she reached for a piece and manoeuvered it towards her mouth.

"No!" exclaimed the Jellyfish. "You can have it, but not eat it too!"

"Why not?" asked Alice, feeling disappointed.

"It wo'n't taste very nice. It has no seasoning," explained the Jellyfish.

"That's a shame," said Alice. "Ca'n't you just add some?"

"No," answered the Jellyfish, "I'm afraid I ca'n't. I got rid of all the seasoning. You see, I'm trying to live always in the now."

It took some consideration for Alice to understand what it meant. Then it struck her. "Oh!" she exclaimed, "You mean you have no spring, summer, fall or winter?"

"I have no spring, summer, *pride*, fall or winter," the Jellyfish corrected her. "Pride comes before the fall, not summer."

Alice remembered she was taught that as well and now wondered how both of these things could be true at the same time—and if they weren't, which of her tutors should be reprimanded. That *would* be something, for her to be able to reprimand her tutor for once, instead of the other way around! She could already see herself putting on a stern face, and waving her index finger at her, while speaking in a firm voice. And then she would make her stand in the corner! No, even better: she would make her copy out Homer's complete Odyssey (as this was the most boring book she could currently think of). Twice!

She was so much looking forward to it, that she had quite forgotten that she had been in the middle of a conversation with the Jellyfish. When she remembered, she quickly asked it: "Is it not very inconvenient to live only in the now?"

"On the contrary," said the Jellyfish, which apparently had not noticed her pause. "As it is July, the waters are always nice and warm and I can forever be on vacation. Also, it keeps the alligators away."

"Well, that's a good thing, I suppose," said Alice, who was now wondering exactly how many alligators there were in this lake, and how big the chances were that she would run into one.

Alice's stomach grumbled again. "Please, Sir," she asked the Jellyfish politely, "would you perhaps have anything that *is* good to eat?"

"Certainly," said the Jellyfish with a good-natured smile. "Just go inside the house. There's always something in the kitchen."

Alice hesitated not a moment and went inside. She had to stoop a bit to get through the front door, but to her surprise it led into a wide hallway. On its walls were shelves attached that reached from the floor to the ceiling. And all shelves were filled to the brim with pies. As Alice walked through the hallway, she saw (and smelled) apple pies, cherry pies, pumpkin pies, cream pies, pecan pies, and many more which she did not immediately recognise. It made her mouth water ("which is a strange thing to do only now—" thought Alice, "—it should have been doing that since the moment I plunged in"), but she expected the Jellyfish to have something even more tasteful in its kitchen.

She tried the first door on her right, but it appeared to be locked. The second door, which was on the left, did open. It was not the kitchen, but another room completely lined from floor to ceiling with shelves holding pies. Alice wondered whether *all* rooms in this house were like this. She closed the door and went back into the hallway. The only option left now was the door at the very end of it. This door also opened and led into a curious kitchen.

The strangest thing was, that the room was so high, she could not see the roof. There were many levels of wooden floors attached to the walls, which had a big hole in the middle so Alice could peer up to them. Kitchens were installed on all floors—at least on the ones she was able to see from down here. "It's like I'm inside a castle's tower, that goes upwards forever!" she thought to herself. "How strange that I wasn't able to see this from the outside! And how tiring it must be for the cooks to swim all the way up each working day, if they work on the highest levels." Alice looked at the shelves of the ground floor kitchen. Instead of pies, they held many ingredients, though she did not recognise all of them. The only place in this kitchen that was not completely stocked up in this way was the kitchen counter, at which a fish was working frantically between stacks of partly completed pies.

"All deliveries in rear!" it shouted when it heard Alice enter, without even looking.

Alice decided to say nothing and wait, and after a while the fish finally turned around to see who it was.

"Oh, hello there," it said, wiping its face with its apron and observing Alice with an inquisitive look. "I'm the Chef de Piscine. Can I help you with something?"

"If you would be so kind," said Alice. "I would like to have something to eat, but I was told the pies don't taste very good. Do you have anything else?"

"I could make you a nice wrap," said the Chef. "I have some cucumber and pickles. I'll be happy to wrap them into this lettuce for you, after I've finished this." It then turned to its counter again and yelled "UP!" which somehow caused the pie it was working on to rise up a level through the opening in the floor. There, it was picked up by one of the other cooks.

Alice eyed the ingredients it had pointed to. They did not look like the cucumber and pickles she knew from home—these ones looked big, slimy, and rather untasty. "I'd prefer something that more resembles pies, if that's possible, please," she said.

The Chef thought about it for a minute. "I could fetch you some puppies, would you like those?"

"Oh, I sure like puppies!" exclaimed Alice, but then realised this was not what the Chef meant, and quickly added: "But I actually meant something to eat."

"You can eat puppies," answered the Chef, without even blinking: "certainly after *I* have prepared them."

"I *can* perhaps, but that doesn't mean I *should*," Alice said in a disapproving tone.

"Wrong," said the Chef. "It's the other way around. For example, I *should* be queen of all of this, but that doesn't mean I *can* be. So, will you have some puppies?"

"DOWN!" came a cry from above. Immediately the Chef moved aside and Alice was only just in time to make room as well for the freshly baked pie that came soaring all the way down the kitchen tower. The door through which Alice had entered flew open all by itself; the pie made a sharp turn when it had almost reached the floor and exited through the door, which then slammed shut behind it.

After having carefully checked the opening in the floors to see whether more pies were arriving, and having established that it was safe again to move, Alice asked the Chef: "Perhaps you have something to drink instead?"

"Certainly," said the Chef, and without stopping stirring in a bowl with its right fin, it reached into one of the cabinets with its other fin, took out a bottle and handed it to Alice. It appeared to be empty.

"I'm sorry," said Alice, "I'm afraid you've given me an empty bottle."

50

"Not at all," said the Chef. "It's completely full. UP!" it cried again, and another partly finished pie rose up to the first level.

Alice looked again at the bottle, but could not see anything in it. With her right hand, she reached for the lid to open it.

"You're holding it upside down!" exclaimed the Chef. "Watch out, or you'll spill it all. And then *you* can clean the ceiling—I have enough to do as it is!"

Startled, Alice immediately let go of the lid. She wondered how it could make the ceiling dirty. "It must be a carbonated drink," she figured, "and the bottle has been shaken a lot." Alice remembered how she had once on a hot summer day tried to open a bottle of carbonated lemonade that she had dropped accidentally, after it had tumbled down a hill. The drink had been *quite* refreshing, but her mother hadn't been very pleased with her appearance afterwards. "But why would it say I'm holding it upside down?" However, Alice did not want to unnecessarily disturb the Chef that was clearly rather busy, so she obediently turned the bottle around—but before opening the lid, she made sure her feet were well out of the way.

When the bottle finally opened, nothing happened, but for a few tiny bubbles escaping from it. She held the bottle above her head to look into it from underneath, but still couldn't see anything inside. "I don't think this will quench my thirst much," she thought. The Chef was still busy with the preparation of another pie, and when it looked the other way, Alice quickly put the bottle between a bunch of other things standing on a corner of the counter, hoping the Chef wouldn't notice. The moment she let go of it, though, the bottle shot upwards through the opening in the floors like a rocket and very soon got out of sight. "UP!" "UP!" "UP!" "UP!" she could hear surprised voices arise from the kitchens above.

To prevent the Chef from noticing, Alice quickly asked it: "May I ask why you are baking so many pies, if they are not very nice to eat?"

"It's just what we do to keep occupied," said the Chef. "And speaking of being occupied—I really have to finish these. And I also still have to cut those into squares before dinnertime." It pointed towards a large stack of root vegetables lying in a corner of the kitchen. "All seventeen hundred and sixty-four of them," it added with a sigh.

Alice looked at the stack of carrots and turnips. It certainly looked like that was going to be a lot of work. "Will it be for pie?" Alice asked, imagining that those weren't going to be tasty either.

"It will be for tea too," replied the chef. "So, if there's nothing else I can help you with—"

"Of course!" cried Alice, "I'll let you get back to work. Thank you for the drink."

"I still think you should have taken the puppies," remarked the Chef.

CHAPTER V

The Well of Fishes

WHEN Alice left the house, the Jellyfish was no longer to be seen. She continued along the path that led away from its house and soon came upon an area that had less vegetation, but was quite crowded with fish. Presently a sad looking codfish swam by. It was holding an umbrella of which only the handle and ribs were left, and it was scouring the lake bottom as if it was looking for something.

"Have you lost something?" asked Alice, who was always eager to help.

"Indeed I have—only I cannot remember what it was," the Codfish answered.

"I hope it wasn't something you were very attached to," said Alice.

"If I were, I wouldn't have lost it, would I?" the Codfish replied contemptuously.

Alice didn't know what to say to that. "May I ask why you are carrying a broken umbrella?" she asked it instead.

"It's not broken," said the Codfish. "It's supposed to look like this."

"But this way it wo'n't protect you from the rain!" Alice said.

"It doesn't need to. It doesn't rain down here, stupid," the Codfish replied.

"I suppose it doesn't," said Alice. "But then, why are you carrying it in the first place?"

The Codfish suddenly looked at Alice as if she had just emerged out of nowhere. "Excuse me, did you say something?"

"I was asking why you are carrying an umbrella if it is not raining."

"Ah, I'm sorry," said the Codfish. "It's just that I'm unschooled. I keep forgetting things within minutes."

"What does being unschooled have to do with your memory?" Alice wondered.

"Everything! Once you leave school, you forget what you used to do!" said the Codfish.

"Why is that?" Alice asked, wondering why no one had told *her* about this. The prospect of undergoing all those lessons, only to forget everything she learned from them the moment they were done, was not something she looked forward to.

"I suppose because you are not allowed to tell tales out of school," it said.

"Would you tell me how come you are unschooled?" inquired Alice.

The Codfish sighed deeply. "I used to attend school. But the school was all about numbers, you see, while I was very bad at mathematics. Fortunately we had a great teacher; I could always count on him. That is, until I really started messing things up." And here the Codfish burst into verse:—

"Three times when adding up primes I was distraught,
  Seven pages homework somehow getting burned,
Nine nights of studying all for naught,
  One error made and not a lesson learned
From the school of Laketown where the cod are taught.
  One Fish to teach them all, One Fish to commend them,
  One Fish to test them all and in the end suspend them
From the school of Laketown where the cod are taught."

"I'm sorry that happened to you," she said.

"What happened to me?" asked the Codfish, who apparently had again forgotten their whole conversation.

"Never mind," said Alice, and walked on.

After a minute or two she came upon a well. On both sides there was a fish angling in it.

"Why would there be a well at the bottom of a lake?" Alice wondered aloud.

"Why wouldn't there be?" responded the Trout on the right.

"Wells are for getting water out of the ground," said Alice. "As there's water all around us here, I'd think there is no need for a well."

"Well, well," mocked the other fish, which appeared to be a Salmon, "we'll see about that."

"We're not trying to get water out of it, child," said the Trout. "We're just fishing in it."

Alice looked puzzled.

"Indeed," the Salmon added. "Why, it would take ages to get all the water out with our hooks! If you think I'm willing to spend so much time on that, you'd better never think again!"

"We're fishing for compliments," the Trout clarified. "Could surely use some of those!"

"So—how are you getting along with that?" asked Alice.

"Not very well," admitted the Trout. "That wretched fish down there keeps stealing our bait. We've tried to reason with it, but it's not very keen."

It took out its line and indeed the hook was empty. From the well arose a sound that resembled a burp, and then a bubble rose up from it.

"Too bad," said the Trout. "That was my last piece of bait." It looked at Alice. "Would you be a dear and go fetch us some new bait?"

Alice did not feel very inclined to run errands for an unfamiliar fish (or for any fish, that was). So she said to the Trout: "I'm very sorry, but being frank, I don't have time for that. I really need to go speak to the Queen Bee, before she sinks my boat!"

"Very well, Frank, then please go fetch us some new bait," said the Trout, not in the least discouraged. "The farm where they sell it is right along the way to the Queen's court. As you pass it anyway, you might as well order some bait for us there. Don't worry, they can deliver it."

"But really, I—" Alice began.

"Just tell them to put it on my bill. Good-bye, Frank!" said the Trout, and turned back to its well and its back to Alice.

It frustrated Alice to be ordered about, but she did not dare protest anymore, as the posture of the fish made it obvious that the conversation had ended. "These creatures are much too full of themselves!" she complained to herself, but set out in the direction of the farm nevertheless.

It did not take her long to find it. As she approached it, she noticed that there were many acres of cultivated ground around the building, on which several fish were working. She decided to take a closer look and walked towards a field that was covered with rocks, which in their turn had shells on them.

"Excuse me," she said to a rather oddly dressed fish (Alice recognised it as a Goby, which she had once seen in an aquarium). He was tapping violently on one of the shells with a stick. "What are you growing here?"

"I'm not growing anything," said the Goby. "They are." He pointed at the shells. "I'm just here to annoy them."

"Why would you annoy them?" exclaimed Alice in a surprised voice.

"Why, to help them grow pearls, of course!" answered the Goby.

"Now I see," said Alice. "These are oysters!"

"Exactly so," said the Goby. "And I'm their caretaker. I used to be the court jester, but the Queen Bee found me more annoying than funny, so she sent me away to work here."

"I'm sorry to hear that," said Alice. "I hope you like your new job as well?"

"Not really," sighed the Goby. "These oysters never applaud me for what I do. Which is rather to be expected, as my boss is only happy if I make them *unhappy*."

Alice thought that was a very sad job indeed. "Perhaps you can entertain me?" she offered, as she felt sorry for the poor fish. "I'm sure you ca'n't be as annoying as the Queen Bee said you were. And I will definitely applaud afterwards, I promise!"

The Goby's face lit up immediately. "Are you sure? Oh, I would love to! What shall I perform, let me think. Ah, I know! I'll recite a poem *and* dance to it! But beware, the poem is rather contro-*vers-ial*, ha ha! I based it on a very familiar one, but it is my own adaptation. Here it goes!"

The Goby straightened himself, filled his lungs and burst into verse. All the while, he made strange movements—he squiggled his fins and tail and kept twisting them to all sides, while still staying almost on the same spot. He turned around his own axis several times—and then Alice thought she saw his head spin on his torso! "But that cannot really have happened," she assured herself. And she tried to focus on the poem again.

58

"'Twas a nightmare, so her loving dad
          Did leave his meeting and he said:
'All mad are all the best of men,
          And return now to bed.'

Beware the monstrous beast, my knight!
          Why, in the end, it should be gone!
Beware the tyrant Queen, and fight
          That freak phenomenon!

She read a scroll and met a cat:
          Long time the story rambled on—
So lay she flat on a giant hat,
          And still it was not done.

And as a croquet game she played,
          A rabbit white, that offered pies,
Made her grow up until she made
          A whale look small in size!

Um, um! Um, um! And who are you?
          The Hatter stood up to the Queen!
He made her sad about her head,
          And disappeared unseen.

'Now shalt thou live up to thy fate?
          Come set us free, here under land!
O you must slay! Right now! This day!'
          They made her understand.

'Twas finished, and so all her fans
          Did clap and brought her back to Dinah;
All thwarted were the wedding plans,
          And she went on to China."

When the Goby had finished his poem, he bowed three times. Then he looked expectantly to Alice.

Alice didn't know what to make of it. To be honest, she couldn't blame the Queen Bee for not liking the Goby's entertainment. "It sounds very pretty," she said, "but it's rather hard to understand!" (You see, she didn't like to confess that she couldn't make sense of it at all.) "Somehow it seems to remind me of something wonderful—only I ca'n't exactly recognise it anymore! However, somebody butchered something, that's clear, at any rate—"

The Goby was still looking at her, seemingly waiting for something. Only then she remembered she had promised him applause, so she quickly put her hands together—although not very convincingly.

"You don't like it either, do you?" sighed the Goby.

"I'm so sorry, I really *tried* to like it," Alice pleaded. "The poetry wasn't even *that* bad," (compared to the dance, she added in her head, as this truthful child did not want to tell a lie). "It just felt—disjointed. And to be honest, I feel that dance was rather unnecessary. It might have been better if you'd left it out altogether."

The Goby sighed even deeper. "I really thought you would find it entertaining. Most young people *do* seem to like it, for some reason."

"Maybe you should try to find something else to do," Alice suggested. "Perhaps you can try growing other pretty things, like water lilies! That may be a more rewarding job."

"I wouldn't know how to," said the Goby. "Which would mean I'd be completely useless and surely would lose my job. Speaking of which—I must go back to work! I've been chatting with you for far too long already."

"Good luck then," said Alice. "I hope you'll eventually be able to find some joy in what you do."

"Thank you. And good-bye," said the Goby rather sadly.

60

The quickest way to reach the farm building was to cross another field. This field was not filled with rocks—instead there were poles in the ground with ropes attached to them, which were floating happily in the current. In the middle of the field there was a fish that looked more like it was *working out* instead of working, as it kept lifting a wooden stick with heavy looking rocks attached on either side of it, above its head.

When the fish noticed Alice, it called out to her: "Ah, you've come to admire my mussels, haven't you?" It swept its face with a towel (although of what use that would be, Alice could not imagine).

"I—I was just wondering what you were doing," faltered Alice, a bit embarrassed.

"I'm training," the fish explained. "I'm a Sport Fish, you see."

"What are you training for?" Alice inquired.

"Why, I'm trying to grow mussels!" it exclaimed. "Ca'n't you see this is a whole field of them?" It pointed at the ropes, on which Alice indeed detected several very small mussels. "It takes time to grow them," the Sport Fish explained. "But within a few months, I will gather them all into a bunch so I can sock them!" It made some boxing moves.

Alice was appalled by the idea. "Oh! You shouldn't hurt those poor defenseless mussels!"

"I wo'n't hurt them," said the Sport Fish, "this is just the way I make them grow stronger."

Alice was not pleased about the process at all. "I was sent here to buy bait—" she said, in an attempt to change the subject, "—but I don't see any here. Am I in the right place?"

"On these fields we are farming. For bait you need to go to the shop. It's right next to the fish nursery inside the building."

"I will do that, thank you," said Alice, and hastily set out for the building once more.

Once she had reached the building and opened the door, an overwhelming cacophony of high pitched shrieks, cries, and yells met her ears. Alice found herself in a large room in which an enormous number of tiny fish was swimming all over the place. Toys and stuffed animals floated everywhere she looked. Several larger fish attempted either to steer the little fish into a certain direction, or to keep them away from something, but their effort appeared to be rather ineffective. Other fish were consoling some little ones, who apparently were crying because they were hurt, frustrated, hungry, or all of that at the same time. (At least, Alice guessed they were crying, as their expressions very much looked like that of her little sister when she was upset. However, she could not actually see any tears, so she assumed they dissolved in the water immediately after they were shed.) The utter chaos and noise baffled Alice and she had to do her best not to turn around and dart out of the building again.

When one of the bigger fish had finally succeeded in separating a tangle of fighting little fish, she was able to spot a door behind them, which had a sign that read "SHOP". Alice made her way towards the door, holding her hands against her ears while being careful not to step on any fish or to walk into them. Two times she had to untangle one from her hair, and she had to make a slight detour because of two fish that were playing hula hoop (with which, Alice realised, were actually rather unhappy looking eels with their tails in their mouths), but in the end she reached the door of the shop and went in.

When she closed the door behind her, the noise dimmed, much to Alice's relief, and she indeed found herself in a small shop. There was a counter, and cupboards containing jars and boxes against the walls behind it. Some of them had labels, like "filters", and "thermometers". For some reason there also was a tall potted plant placed directly behind the counter. On the floor to the right she saw a large barrel with a sign saying "Sponges: now 30% off!", and in a corner several hammocks were put up. But what caught Alice's attention most were the glass cases on the left of the counter. They contained the most beautiful pearls she had ever seen: big, shiny pearls lying on cushions, as well as pieces of jewellery that were made from them. Alice walked towards the cases and pressed her nose against the glass to give them a closer look. "Why, that necklace is fit for a queen!" she exclaimed in admiration.

"Thank you," a small voice said.

Alice hastily took a step back. The voice seemed to have come from the direction of the counter, but except for the potted plant, she could see nothing behind it. And the only thing on top of it was a pretty little treasure chest, which opened its lid every few seconds to let out bubbles of air.

"Excuse me," she asked: "But who just spoke to me?"

The plant rustled a bit, and then she could see a fish's face emerging from the bushes. First, it was only a set of lips that protruded. Then, very slowly, more of the face appeared between the leaves, until Alice was able to distinguish eyes peering through the shrubbery as well. "Me. The shopkeeper," the fish said timidly.

"I almost did not notice you there!" said Alice in a surprised voice. "Why are you hiding in a plant?"

"I'm a little shy—" the Shopkeeper responded.

"Isn't that somewhat inconvenient for some one in your profession?" Alice asked with a frown.

"Yes," it simply replied.

As no other explanation followed, Alice decided to just go ahead. "Well, I don't mean to frighten you. I was sent to order bait. Can I buy some from you?"

"What kind of bait?" the Shopkeeper inquired.

"I—I don't know, to be honest," Alice admitted. "They did not specify."

"Well, let's see," said the Shopkeeper in a somewhat more confident voice. "We have several types of bait. Which one you need depends on what you will be using it for." Its face retracted into the plant and there was some rustling. Then, the whole plant moved towards one of the cupboards. There was some more rustling, and the plant returned. A fin holding a large glass jar emerged from it. "For example, this—" the Shopkeeper's voice sounded, a bit muffled between the greenery, "—is clickbait. It's cheap, but not always appropriate. You mainly use it for catfishing." When it got no confirming response from Alice, the jar disappeared into the plant again. The plant was being shoved towards another cupboard, and upon return the fin emerged again, this time holding a large box. "Will you be fishing with reels? Then you could use pipers. I can guarantee these are very good quality; they are very fast!"

"I'm not sure," said Alice. "They told me they are fishing for compliments. What should they use for that?"

"Ah, in that case they'll need suckers," said the Shopkeeper. "Unfortunately we're all out." And before Alice even had time to blink, the fish had emerged from the plant, grabbed a little notebook from behind the counter, and retracted into the plant again. "I see I'll be getting another batch on the fifth—so that would be tomorrow," it sounded from within the bush. "I can put an order in for you now and ship 'em once they arrive, if you like?"

"Well, if there's no other option, I suppose that will do," said Alice, who did not feel very responsible for the Trout's bait. "If it didn't want that, it should have gone here himself!" she thought

defiantly, and to the Shopkeeper she said: "It's for the Trout that is fishing in the well over there. Do you know it? Can you put the order on its bill?"

"I know him," said the Shopkeeper, of which Alice could now only see its moving lips, "but if you know he's a trout, you should also know he doesn't have a bill. And I wo'n't give him a loan anymore either—he only feigns interest, and I sha'n't have anymore of that. He can pay on delivery."

"That will be fine," said Alice, relieved that there was another option, and turned around with the intention to leave.

Just at that moment, the door opened and another customer, which Alice recognised as a tuna, entered the shop, accompanied by great noise from the other room. "Hello there, Molly!" he shouted towards the plant, while he tried to close the door. However, he was unable to do so because of a tiny fish with swimming wings that had emerged. It seemed to be adrift and floated helplessly through the door opening, frantically wiggling its little tail. A few seconds later a landing net swooshed in, which caught the little fish and dragged it back into the nursery (just like the people you sometimes see being pulled off the stage by a hook). The tuna fish quickly shut the door, scraped his throat, and addressed the plant. "I'd like some bait!"

"Certainly, Tunny," replied the Shopkeeper, protruding its lips from the vegetation again. "What would you like to catch? I didn't know you were interested in fishing."

"Oh, it's not so much that I want to *catch* anything," said the Tuna. "I merely want to *lure* something."

"All right. Then what would you like to lure?" asked the Shopkeeper.

"The moon," replied the Tuna.

There was a silence.

"I'm not sure what bait you'll need for that," hesitated the Shopkeeper.

"Neither am I," sighed the Tuna. "I was hoping you'd be able to tell me. Well, give me a bit of everything then. I'll just have to experiment."

Alice watched while the plant seemed to drag itself to several cupboards. After some time it returned, and eight little bags with wares got thrown out of the plant onto the counter. The Tuna picked them up and forcefully threw some coins towards the plant, then turned and left.

Alice watched him leave. "Why would he want to *lure the moon*?" she asked, very much intrigued.

"Oh, don't ask me, I only know about bait. Go ask him—he's a lunartic," answered the lips of the Shopkeeper. It then fully disappeared into the vegetation again and the plant went completely silent.

When nothing more happened, Alice left the shop and, once outside, could just see the Tuna swim around a corner. "Please, Sir," she called out to him. "Please wait!" And burning with curiosity, she ran after him.

CHAPTER VI

The Lunartic

ALICE turned the corner just in time to see the Tuna disappear into an opening in a rock. After climbing the rock and following him through the crevice, she found herself in a large cave with a big rectangular table in the middle. The walls and the table were covered with papers, showing complex formulas, charts and drawings she did not understand. There was a clock on the wall that indicated it was twenty-eight minutes past eleven ("Which cannot be correct," Alice thought—she was sure it had to be at least two hours later, as it was far past lunch time already). Alice felt she was intruding, but as there was no door, she had not been able to knock. She took a few steps back to check whether there was a bell on the outside of the rock, but as there was none there either, she hesitantly went back inside and cleared her throat.

"I'm very sorry to just barge into your office," said Alice, a bit ashamed, "but there is no door."

The Tuna put his purchases on the table and looked at Alice. "I'm aware there isn't one. Why should there be?"

"Well," said Alice, "there does not necessarily have to be a door, but now there is nothing to knock on, you see. And neither is there a bell to ring."

"Are you a musician?" asked the Tuna.

"A musician? No, not at all," said Alice. "I just wanted to announce my arrival."

"And why would you want to do that?" asked the Tuna.

"So you know I am here," answered Alice.

"I already know you are here," said the Tuna, "as I can see you stand there. If I *did* have a door, I *wouldn't* be able to see you, as you would be on the other side of it. Really, you are making this far more complicated than necessary."

Alice did not know what to say to that, but at least the fish did not seem to mind her being there. So she asked him: "I could not help overhearing your question in the shop. Please, would you tell me why you are trying to lure the moon, and where to?"

The Tuna's face lightened up with a big smile. "You are interested in my studies? Please, come in!" he said. "I never get any visitors, especially so late in the evening!" He shoved aside some of the papers to make room and pulled out a small stool from under the table. "Please, sit!"

"Are you a scientist?" Alice asked, admiring one of the papers on the table, on which she recognised the waterline of the lake and the moon, and a lot of arrows pointing in several directions.

"Definitely!" said the Tuna. "In fact, I am a biologist, physicist, astronomer, *and* economist. My job is to increase the productivity in this lake, you see."

Alice was impressed. "It must have taken lots of lessons to become all of that," she said.

"Ah, but I'm completely self-taught!" replied the Tuna proudly.

"How exactly are you trying to accomplish this productivity increase?" Alice inquired. "And how does it involve the moon?"

"Well, I've tried several strategies," answered the Tuna. "But until now, the most viable one seems to involve spring tide. That's when the inhabitants of this lake seem to be the most active. Unfortunately, it does not occur very often. And as it is currently summer, it will take a long time for it to occur again. That's why I'm trying to find a way to increase its frequency."

"That sounds complicated," said Alice, who wasn't looking forward to a lengthy explanation of the process. "But I don't see how that involves the moon."

"It is very complicated, indeed!" said the Tuna boastfully. "I'm sure I'm the only one who can do it. There is no other fish in this lake as clever as I am! Let me try to explain in a way you can understand."

Alice did not like his condescending tone, but decided to say nothing and wait for him to continue.

"My theory was that spring tides have something to do with the stars and the planets. So I have been studying them in depth," the Tuna started. He pointed towards a corner of the cave, where a very strange creature was tied to a rope. It had the tail of a fish, but the head and the front legs of a goat, and it was trying to munch on some plants that were growing through a large crack in the cave wall. However, as the rope it was tied with was rather short, it had trouble reaching them, and it seemed to be rather uncomfortable. Above the goat-fish, two koi were continuously swimming in circles. They appeared to be joined together with each one's tail tied to the head of the other.

"Those poor creatures!" thought Alice.

"After many explorations, I finally discovered that during spring tide, the moon and the sun are aligned with our planet," continued the Tuna. "So to create more spring tides, I figured I must get them to align more often. At first I tried making an artificial sky." He pointed towards another corner of the cave, where he had caged a lanternfish. A piece of cheese was lying on the ground and several starfish had attached themselves to the wall.

"Unfortunately, they were not bright enough." (Alice thought she heard some muttering sounds arise from the corner.) "So I decided to teach them. Alas, my attempts were unsuccessful; they never got any better."

"What did you try to teach them?" Alice asked.

"Oh, all kinds of things," said the Tuna.

From the corner came some very small, muffled voices. "We know a song!" one of them said. "A pretty one!" said another. "Would you like to hear?" asked a third.

"Oh yes, I would very much like to," said Alice, who correctly guessed it were the Starfish that had spoken. She got up and walked towards the corner.

"The song is called '*Aquariums*'," one of them said. It produced a note, on which the others all chimed in. Then they started singing:—

> *"When the winter has departed*
> *   Then shellfish will in scattershot*
> *Release their eggs with offspring*
> *   In water that's nice and hot*
>
> *This is the spawning of the clams in aquariums*
> *The clams in aquariums*
> *Aquariums!*
> *Aquariums!*
>
> *Walls of glass as their surrounding*
> *Muddy earth provides their founding*
> *No more hiding between dishes*
> *In the company of fishes*
> *Pebbles, sand and rock formation*

Overgrown with vegetation
Aquariums!
Aquariums!

When the winter has departed
*   Then shellfish will in scattershot*
Release their eggs with offspring
*   In water that's nice and hot*

This is the spawning of the clams in aquariums
The clams in aquariums
Aquariums!
Aquariums!"

"That was lovely!" applauded Alice, when the song had finished. "Actually, I think you are *very* bright, to be able to sing so beautifully. The Tuna has taught you well!" The Starfish started glowing with pride. "Although I'm not at all surprised that he couldn't teach it to the cheese," Alice added, giggling.

"And why is that?" an offended voice came from the floor. "Do you feel better than me?"

Alice looked down in surprise. Indeed, it was the piece of cheese that had spoken to her. "You fish and humans think you are all so superior," it continued, furiously. "Just because you have a brain and I don't. That's discrimination, I say! My grandmother was a cow, and cows have brains. We have the same kind of ancestors, only I have evolved differently over the course of time. That does not make me any less than you. Pah!"

"I'm very sorry," said Alice to the Cheese. "I did not mean to offend you. I did not know you could hear what I said."

"So that makes it all right?" exclaimed the Cheese. "If I am not able to hear it—it is all right to say nasty things about me?" Its voice was becoming a bit sluggish.

"No," said Alice hastily, "that's not what I meant! I meant, I also did not know you could speak. Or think."

"Exactly!" fumed the cheese. "You did not think I could think, because—you look down on me! Because I don't have a brain. Discrimination—I tell you!"

"I—I—" faltered Alice, who realised she was only making things worse and had no idea how to calm down the Cheese, which was getting more and more hot-headed by the minute. She noticed that sweat was starting to drip from its sides. Alice also thought it was beginning to look a bit wobbly.

"The only thing—that we are—good for—is being—eaten!" the Cheese went on, ever more slowly. "Don't—you——think—" And then it stopped shouting. Its body was becoming liquid and began to pour over the floor, until all that was left was a puddle of melted cheese. Startled, Alice took several steps back.

"Never mind, I'll clean that up later," said the Tuna, who did not seem to care a bit. "Anyway," he continued his explanation, as if nothing had happened, "after that plan had failed, I decided to try moving the actual moon. I realised the sun would be too hot to touch, you see, so it would be best to try shoving the moon instead." While Alice walked back to the table, still a bit shocked because of what had happened to the Cheese, he fumbled through a stack of papers and took out a large sheet of paper that showed a blueprint of a tall contraption. "See, this was my design for a ladder. Unfortunately, the thing collapsed before it was high enough. Must have been the dry air up there. So I came up with yet another brilliant plan. I thought, if I could just *lure* the moon into the right position, there'd be no need for shoving. And it would save me a lot of trouble as well! Clever, ain't it? Now I only need to find out what it likes. That's the project I'm currently working on."

"Now I understand why you need bait," said Alice. "I hope at least one of those you bought attracts it. But how will you be offering it to the moon?"

"That's the easy part," said the Tuna. "I just need a very long pole with a rope and hook."

"Where would you get such a long pole?" Alice wanted to know.

"Of course I have thought about that as well," said the Tuna. "I planted bamboo two days ago. Bamboo grows really fast, you know. I calculated the exact spot and angle in which it needs to grow. This morning I attached a rope and hook to it, and tomorrow I will add some of this bait to the hook. And then I only have to wait until it has grown high enough. Clever, ain't it?"

"Are you sure that's going to work?" asked Alice, rather doubtfully.

"Not yet," said the Tuna. "But they say the proof is in the pudding!" Upon that, he took out a large bowl of pudding from underneath the table and put it upside down on his head with so much force that drops of pudding flew everywhere. Alice wiped some of it off her face and stuck her finger into her mouth. It tasted quite good.

"You have to let it sink in a bit first!" said the Tuna very earnestly, while pudding was trickling down his face. "By the way, would you mind helping me put up some pamphlets?" He rummaged through a stack of papers and pulled out several blank ones. On them, he wrote "MAD MOCK MOONS MAY MELT" and signed them with his name.

"What's that for?" Alice wanted to know.

"Why, I need to publish my findings," said the Tuna, while wiping away some drops of pudding that had fallen onto the top of the stack. "All scientists need to publish, you know, or we wo'n't get funding for our research. So I am publishing my research result of to-day."

"But who needs to know this?" asked Alice. "How is this relevant to anybody else?"

"That's not important," said the Tuna. "Everyone knows that the more you publish, the better a scientist you are. Obviously you don't know much about science! Also, as I am funded by the

Queen, I have a social responsibility to educate those who are not blessed with an IQ as high as mine."

Alice bit her cheek. "Actually, shouldn't my name be on these as well? After all, I was the one who made it melt. Without my help, you wouldn't have discovered it."

"Certainly not," said the Tuna indignantly. "It all happened under *my* supervision."

Alice thought that was completely unfair. "On the other hand," she considered, "it might not at all be a good idea to publicly announce that I made something so mad it turned into a puddle. Who knows, they might even arrest me for murder!—Although I've heard it is very hard to get convicted if there is no body."

74

Nevertheless, Alice decided that she'd rather not take the chance and didn't press the matter on.

"It is fortunate that you are here, though," the Tuna continued, "because I also have to present my paper about the subject. So here you go, you can have this one for free." And with a solemn look on his face, he pressed one of the copies into Alice's hands with both his fins and bowed, causing droplets of pudding to fall onto the floor and the paper. "Now, help me put up the rest of them."

The Tuna then handed her half of the remaining stack of pamphlets and swam outside with the other half, still wearing the bowl of pudding on his head. Alice was about to follow him out of the cave, when she changed her mind. Quickly she ran towards the corner where the goat-fish and the koi were held, and untied their ropes. All three immediately swam away through the crack in the rock. She then continued to the other corner and opened the cage that held the lanternfish, which did not hesitate to follow the others. "There you go," thought Alice. "And I think the Starfish can find their way out themselves if they want to." She exited through the large opening herself. "Now, where to put up those pamphlets?"

First she tried attaching one to the wall of the cave, but realised she had nothing to make it stay up there. "I could use some tape or pins," she thought, and turned around to see how the Tuna was managing it. She was just in time to see him stick one under the fin of a passing bass. Next, he started folding another into a boat, which he then threw away from him, so it drifted along with the current. Alice decided to just lay a pamphlet on the ground and place a stone on top of it, so it would not float away. She continued walking into the direction the Queen's court was supposed to be, and every couple of yards, put one of the pamphlets on the ground. Once more she looked back. In the distance she could see the Tuna using a poor sea urchin to pin his pamphlet to a piece of driftwood.

CHAPTER VII

Say it with Tentacles

AFTER Alice had fixed her last copy to the lake bottom, she noticed movement in the distance. It turned out to be a group of octopuses, that were creating all kinds of figures with their tentacles. It looked as if they were dancing, as all of them moved and held their tentacles elegantly in different shapes, or formed symmetrical shapes together. Along with their movements, their skins were continuously changing in colour, as if they were chameleons. "How magnificent!" Alice exclaimed, and clapped.

The octopuses immediately froze mid-air (or mid-water—that would be the right term here, Alice thought) and then tried to flee. But as their tentacles had been intertwined and they all tried to flee in different directions, they got hopelessly entangled instead. The previously graceful octopuses instantly morphed into a giant ball of protrusions, that continued wriggling for almost half a minute. Then, all of a sudden, a dark cloud emanated from somewhere inside the ball and completely engulfed them.

For a moment, nothing more seemed to happen. Alice could only see the cloud hanging still in the water, as if it was a thunderstorm. Then, it slowly began to dissolve and the tangled heap of octopuses sank to the bottom of the lake. It landed with a little thump, upsetting the sand underneath it. The octopuses apparently had managed to entangle themselves so badly that they now weren't able to move anymore at all, and the only thing they could do was watch Alice with a stupefied look on their faces.

"Oh, I'm so sorry to have scared you!" cried Alice. "Here, let me help you!" She ran towards the heap and started randomly pulling on tentacles, trying to untie all the knots. It took her a while, but once she had succeeded in loosening the first tentacle, it became easier to undo the others. Slowly, one by one, she managed to untangle all the octopuses again.

"I'm really very sorry," Alice said again, after she had undone the last knot—which was a tentacle from the largest octopus that had wrapped itself around the head of the smallest one twice before wrapping around itself, and had then suctioned itself so firmly to its own skin that it refused to come loose until Alice had decided to tickle it. "I only wanted to applaud for your beautiful show!"

"That was not a show, child," said the largest Octopus, who seemed to be considered the leader among them. "We were communicating in our native language. In fact, we were singing a traditional song."

"That is certainly an interesting way to communicate," said Alice. "Do all octopuses communicate like that? I mean, all octopi. No, wait–" hesitated Alice, feeling confused. (To her great dismay she could not remember which was the correct plural form.)

"It's 'octopuses', child. You shouldn't change 'us' into 'I', for then we wouldn't be a team," the large Octopus said.

"And yes, we have to be creative," said another Octopus, stretching its tentacles, "as we have ink, but no pens to write with."

"Could you please say something to me in tentacle language?" Alice begged excitedly.

78

"I'm afraid you wouldn't understand our language." said the large Octopus. "But we can form shapes with our tentacles that you'll be able to recognise. Here, let me form some words for you in your own language." It drifted to about ten feet in the air (water, Alice corrected herself again) and began to create letters by bending its tentacles and holding several of them together. It took Alice only a few seconds to recognise them:

"I'm fine, thank you." said Alice, delighted. "Oh, I didn't think I would be able to read this so easily!"

The Octopus signed again:

"Thank you!" Alice cried. "No, wait—let me try to say that in tentacle shapes as well!" And eagerly she started fumbling with her arms to create letters. From the corner of her eye she saw two other Octopuses nudge each other and chortle. Alice ignored them.

"This wo'n't do at all," she muttered to herself, after having made several vain attempts. "I declare that I don't have enough arms for this," she eventually concluded in a disappointed tone.

By now, the two other Octopuses had started to laugh loudly at Alice's attempts, but a third Octopus put them in their place: "Before you two start commenting on the attempts of others," it remarked in a scornful tone, "you both should learn to properly stretch your tentacles all the way. You were holding them all curled up during the song."

"Yes, and only a sucker would think that he did well at the part where we had to hold onto each other to form a circle!" cried a fourth. "My tentacles are still hurting!"

"Girls!" reprimanded the large Octopus. "Let's discuss this during our next rehearsal, shall we?" It turned its attention to Alice again. "Will you join us in a game of charaoke?"

"What is charaoke?" Alice asked in a surprised voice. "I've never heard of such a thing!"

"Do you know karaoke?" asked the Octopus.

"Yes, I do," said Alice.

"And do you know charades?"

"Yes, my sisters and I sometimes play that at home."

"Well, then you should also know what charaoke is!" the Octopus exclaimed. "Come on!"

Upon that, the Octopuses split up into two groups. One group depicted shapes representing characters and scenes with their tentacles, while the other group tried to guess them and then sang them. It all happened so very fluently that it appeared to Alice as if they already knew the lyrics, but this was probably because the Octopuses proved to be so *very* good at portraying things. Even she could make out the lyrics most of the time, and as the tune was very easy to remember, she found herself loudly singing along with the rest of her group before she knew it:—

"There once was a fireman living in need
Who did not receive any raise.
He found all his future plans being too dark,
And started to see in a haze.
Together our tentacles thus will portray
Him trying to light up the place.

There once was a linesman who genuinely thought
That safety rules were poppycock.
So surely he didn't adhere to them all
When fixing his car's engine block.
Together our tentacles thus will portray
Him grasping their value in shock.

There once was a goldfish immensely concerned
About drought and its long term duration.
He noticed his water resolve into air
Which caused him tremendous frustration.
Together our tentacles thus will portray
Him fearing prolonged dehydration.

There once was a chauffeur who, steering his bus
    Quite lacked a trajectory notion.
He found himself driving along on the beach
    His wheels almost touching the ocean.
Together our tentacles thus will portray
    Him risking impending demotion.

There once was a client who went to the barber
    Considering talking a sport.
So even the hairdresser failed to chime in,
    And nothing could make him abort.
Together our tentacles thus will portray
    Them cutting his long frizzles short.

There once was a bird who was singing out loud
    For which he acquired great fame.
His flock member then interrupted his show
    With melodies nearly the same.
Together our tentacles thus will portray
    Him filing a copyright claim.

There once was a seamstress whose customer asked
To sew him a new pair of breeches.
He found, when he suddenly slid off his horse,
She'd covered a lot of her glitches.
Together our tentacles thus will portray
Her clientele being in stitches.

There once was a wrinkly and grey engineer
Who thought himself awfully clever.
Convinced he was able to build a machine
That lengthened his living forever.
Together our tentacles thus will portray
Him failing his fruitless endeavour.

There once was an old man whose dream it had been
To live out his life a king's vassal.
But after his wish had come true, realised
He found it too much of a hassle.
Together our tentacles thus will portray
Him atop his inflatable castle.

There once was a businessman fearing his funds
  Were quickly depleting in size.
He found his dyslexia hindering him,
  Their sales reports hurted his eyes.
Together our tentacles thus will portray
  Him trying to capitalise.

There once was a painter world-famous because
  In numerous colours he drew.
He knew his commissions came in from the mob,
  But overdrew what he could do.
Together our tentacles thus will portray
  Them leaving him all black and blue.

There once was a pig absolutely convinced
  He was in fact able to fly.
So often the saying was uttered out loud
  He might as well give it a try.
Together our tentacles thus will portray
  His relatives waving good-bye."

After the song was over, everyone cheered. "And now we switch places!" the grey Octopus cried.

"Oh, I would love to keep playing, but I'm afraid I don't have enough time for it," Alice said with a feeling of regret. "I really need to be on my way again, as I have to speak to the Queen Bee. Do you perhaps know which way I should go to find her?"

"I think it is *that* way," replied the large Octopus, pointing with only the tip of its tentacle. "But that road may take you dangerously close to the Scuttleflot. I can hear it right now!"

Alice listened intently. And indeed she could hear a small bang!, followed by a splash of water in the distance.

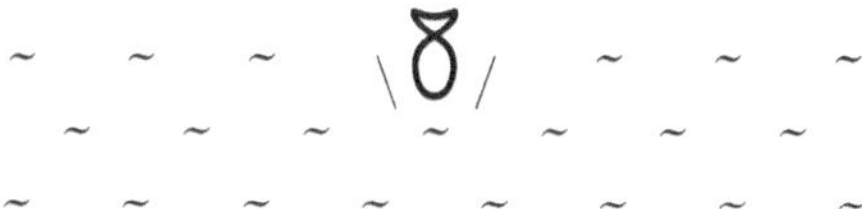

"Well, I shall see then which path to take—I may be going to take a detour," said Alice.

She was hardly startled by the shell propelling upwards—by now she had got used to it doing so whenever she said something after hearing a splash, although she still could not quite understand why it happened. Alice said her good-byes to the Octopuses, who continued their game without her, and went on her way. She decided to take the path despite the Octopus' warning. Perhaps if she was really careful and quiet, the Scuttleflot might not spot her.

Luckily the path she was following was quite overgrown. "Which means nobody will be able to see me from a distance," thought Alice. "But then, if the Scuttleflot is not able to dive, it will spot me from above! I will need to hide the top of my head." She looked around and decided to pick several large strands of grass, and weave them into a little crown, just as she did when making a daisy chain. "There," she said, while placing it onto her head: "that should provide some camouflage! But I will also need to make sure it wo'n't hear me."

So she continued on her way as silently as possible, trying to avoid stepping on sticks and stones, when Alice realised that there was actually quite a lot of noise coming from up ahead. It did not sound as if it was from a monster, but she kept very quiet nevertheless. (Of course, Alice had not actually ever *heard* a monster, so she could not be absolutely certain that this wasn't the sound of one. There was once a time when she had *thought* that she had heard a monster, when she was lying in bed and had noticed strange noises coming from underneath it. But after she had called for her mother, who had then looked bravely under the bed to chase it away, it had turned out just to be one of their kittens who was still trying to figure out how to purr properly.)

As Alice came closer, she began to hear voices over the noise. "It sounds as if they are building something over there," she thought. And indeed, when she carefully peeked behind a heap of sand from which the noise seemed to originate, she saw two sharks and a swordfish working on a *very* awkward looking construction.

Alice quickly drew her head back. Although it was neither the Scuttleflot, nor another monster, she figured that drawing the attention of sharks was not a bright idea either—especially since she was now so small, compared to them. So she decided to stay hidden behind the heap of sand for a while to observe them. Perhaps an opportunity to sneak past them unseen would present itself.

Alice tiptoed to the other side of the heap, where a cluster of large plants were growing. They were dense enough to hide her from sight, yet she could still watch the sharks through the gaps between their stems. From this side, she was able to get a better look at the building as well. It was a strange building indeed—not a single wall seemed to be straight, the door appeared to be located on the roof, and there was some kind of vertical balcony sticking out of one of the sides.

Near Alice, there was a large pile of construction wood, and the Swordfish was swimming into its direction. She crouched to the

ground in order to hide herself better. While the Swordfish was rummaging through the pile of wood, apparently looking for a suitable piece, Alice suddenly felt something crawling upon her leg. Startled, she looked down, and discovered a little creature making its way up her calf. At that very moment, another one jumped onto her, and she spotted even more tiny creatures emerging from the sand all round her. Unable to contain herself, she jumped up in alarm and began screaming, while desperately kicking her leg, trying to get the creatures off. She tumbled through the bushes and fell to the ground—straight in front of the Swordfish.

"Please, don't hurt me! I am no threat to you" pleaded poor Alice. "And I don't taste nice at all either!" she added quickly, eyeing the sharks.

The Swordfish looked at her, but made no attempt to attack. "I wo'n't hurt you, if you wo'n't hurt our pensioners. Be careful, you're almost crushing them."

Alice looked to her side, where both her grass crown and the Sand Fleas (as which she was finally able to identify the creatures, now that she could take a good look at them) had fallen. "Your—your pensioners?"

"Yes," said the Swordfish. "*This* one," it pointed to the Sand Flea nearest to her, "is president of the board emerita. She oversaw the quality of our material. And *this* one," it continued, pointing to the other Sand Flea, "is our chairwoman emerita. She was in charge of interior design. The best we ever had!"

"I'm truly sorry, I did not intend to hurt them," said Alice. "They just gave me quite a scare."

The Sand Fleas were already burying themselves in the sand again. Before the Swordfish could reply, one of the Sharks, which had a wide, blunt face in the shape of a hammer, shouted: "Get back to work, you old chatterbug, or we'll never finish this thing in time! Fetch me another beam!"

"All right, all right!" muttered the Swordfish, and shoved a piece of wood towards the other Shark, whose job it apparently was to saw the wood into the right size.

"How long should this beam be sawn?" the Saw-Shark asked the other Shark.

The Hammerhead Shark showed its blueprint, which indicated 10″.

The Saw-Shark randomly chose a spot on the beam, and counted while sawing. When it had counted to ten, it stopped, although it had sawn only about halfway through.

"And how wide should it be?" it asked then.

The Hammerhead Shark looked at its blueprint again. Alice noticed it indicated a width of 2′. "Uhm, it says... two prime...?"

The Saw-Shark shook its head. "Not relevant, we'll be priming the beams only after we've attached them. Let's skip that part."

Alice hesitatingly interrupted: "I'm not quite sure that is correct..."

The Swordfish sighed. "It's all so complicated! We lived here long before the Queen Bee took over and all this became imperial grounds. It is taking us quite some time to get used to her standards. For example, she wants her yard to be only three feet long! Can you imagine?"

"Actually, my point is—" Alice began to say, but then she heard a rustling sound not far away, originating from some bushes. "What is that?" she asked in an alarmed voice, still a bit shaken by the thought of the Scuttleflot being near, encountering sharks and being crawled by creatures all within minutes.

"An ounce is under a stone—" the Swordfish mumbled distractedly.

"Is it trapped?" Alice asked in alarm. "It will be dangerous if it is hurt!"

The Swordfish looked at her incomprehensibly. Then, a tiny guppy emerged from the bushes. Alice took a relieved breath. "It was only a guppy making that noise! Not an ounce!"

"I never said it was," said the Swordfish.

Meanwhile, the Hammerhead Shark was pounding nails into the beam the Saw-Shark had prepared for it. Each time it took a nail from its toolkit, sounds seemed to emerge from it. Alice walked towards the kit for a closer inspection—"for if something happens to be trapped in there, I should free it!"

And indeed, as soon as the Hammerhead Shark took out another nail, several small voices cried out again: "There it goes! Get ready all of you, *this is not a drill!*—I might be next! Somebody pinch me!—Yes! He nailed it!—No need to tell me; I *saw* that!—

Whiner. I'm only getting down to your level, you know.—Oh, you're such a tool!—Well, screw you!"

But before Alice could take a better look at the contents of the toolkit, she got interrupted by the arrival of a cobbler fish. For some reason he was wearing shoes on two of his lower fins.

"All of you!" the Cobbler called out stiffly, demanding everybody's attention. "I was sent by the Queen to inspect this building. Move aside!"

The four of them obeyed.

"Why is he wearing shoes?" Alice whispered to the Swordfish. "I would think he doesn't need any. Also, they look *very* worn."

"I think it's a status sign," the Swordfish ans-wered softly. "He wears shoes, which implies that he has two feet. While we merely have a couple of gills. I'd say he's showing off!"

The Cobbler was looking back and forth from the blueprints to the construction. "This is all wrong. There's a fault in the foundations of your building," he concluded.

"Darn," said the Hammerhead Shark. "I knew we should have checked it twice."

"All right. That would be all. Go on with your work," said the Cobbler and swam away. The Sharks picked up their tools again and continued from where they had left off.

"Wait, are you not going to make any corrections?" asked Alice.

"Decidedly not!" exclaimed the Saw-Shark. "We leave it exactly as it is. The Queen has made it *very* clear that she requires us to be loyal to a fault. And we're not about to disobey her and make her angry—nohow!"

"I see," said Alice. "Then I suppose it is the right thing to do. Now, I don't want to keep you from your work, so I will continue on my way. I am going to visit the Queen Bee, you know!"

The Saw-Shark looked at her doubtfully. "You'll have to be careful. This is a dangerous area. Not the ideal place for a little girl like you to wander alone."

"I'm afraid I don't have much choice," said Alice. "I really need to see the Queen and I don't know how else I can get to her. And I have no one to join me."

The Saw-Shark nodded. "Well then, at least take the safest path—go straight ahead here, and when you reach the crossing, you'll have to make a left turn. First, take route 4 and route 16. Cross some squares with two trees. When you've done that, just take route 36. Meaning it will clearly show you the right way!"

"Thank you very much," said Alice, and waved to the three of them as she left.

CHAPTER VIII

An Unpleasant Encounter

AFTER having followed the path for several minutes, a large dark shape loomed up in front of Alice. It had parts sticking out to all sides. Only when she came closer, she recognised the dark shape as a big ship that had sunk to the lake bottom. The parts that stuck out were broken masts—of the sails, no more than a couple of frayes were left. "Oh dear," thought Alice, "this must have been from another poor soul who was unaware of the Queen Bee and her Scuttleflot!" Indeed, there was a large hole in the bow, as if the boat had been torpedoed. Alice intended to walk past it quickly, but when she had barely reached the front of the ship, she heard shouting.

"Arrr! Stop right there, you land-lubber! Prepare to be boarded!"

The sound appeared to originate from inside the wreck. Alice looked more closely and saw a triggerfish swimming through the hole in the bow. It was wearing a black tricorn hat and a leather eye patch over its left eye—she almost missed the eye patch because the triggerfish also had a large black spot on its belly, which looked exactly like the patch.

The Triggerfish approached and spoke again, this time rather politely instead of shouting: "Now, lass, would you mind entering that little shack over there?"

Alice looked over her shoulder to a wooden frame that was timbered with planks and had a small opening on one side, with some spare planks and nails lying next to it. "Why?" she asked.

"Because I need to board you," the Triggerfish replied. "But you don't have your own ship—like most who pass here," it added with a sigh. "So I need to improvise."

"I'd rather not, if you don't mind," said Alice. "Actually I do have a ship—although it's merely a rowing boat. I'm on my way to the Queen Bee, because I don't want it to end up like yours."

"What's wrong with my ship?" the fish asked in an offended voice.

"Well, it's got quite a hole in it, which I assume is the reason it sank," Alice said matter-of-factly.

"It's good enough for me!" the Triggerfish said stubbornly. "All I ever wanted is to be a pirate. I don't care whether my ship is *under* water or *on* the water!"

"You're a pirate!" Alice exclaimed. "How exciting! I've never met a pirate before. I've only read about them in stories!"

(Although she had read that pirates were supposed to be fearsome, she wasn't frightened a bit by this one. After all, she supposed, this was a rather ordinary fish, without sharp teeth or a pointy nose, and a good deal smaller than she was.)

"Aye, so did I," said the Triggerfish. "I used to live in an aquarium. My owners read many stories to their children, which I was able to overhear, and I liked those about pirates best. So I decided to become one!"

"How did you manage to escape from the aquarium and get your own ship?" Alice wanted to know.

"I pretended to be dead. Then they flushed me down the toilet and I ended up here," said the Triggerfish. "I found this ship just lying here on the bottom of the lake. As there was no owner to be seen, I claimed it. So now it is my pirate ship!"

Alice clapped her hands. "It's so great that you were able to fulfil your dream!"

"Isn't it?" asked the Triggerfish. "Well now, seeing as this boarding thing isn't going the way I planned it, let's leave it for what it is and skip right to the pillaging, shall we? What valuables do you have on you?"

"I'm afraid I don't have anything that is worth stealing," said Alice. "And I don't exactly appreciate being robbed."

"Sorry, but it comes with the job, you know," said the Triggerfish, a little embarrassed.

Alice looked at it. It looked more laughable than threatening with the hat and the eye patch, and she could not imagine how it was going to enforce anything on her. So she folded her arms and decidedly said: "I understand that, but you cannot make me give you my belongings."

The Triggerfish hesitated for a moment, and then suddenly shouted: "Look behind you, a three-headed monkey!"

"If you're trying to distract me: it isn't working," said Alice in a reproachful tone. "I wo'n't hand over my belongings, and I wo'n't let you grab them when I'm not looking either!"

The Triggerfish sighed. "All right—I see I cannot fool you, and you clearly have the advantage here, as you're the only one of us who is armed. That's not usually the case with the creatures passing here. I just thought I'd give it a try anyway. Or else I wouldn't be a proper pirate, would I?—But I suppose I really *do* need to find me a sword," it added, contemplatively.

It looked so disappointed that Alice began to feel sorry for the fish. "Come now," she thought, "there must be *some* way to make it happy." She thought about it for a minute and then fumbled through her apron pockets. There was not much in them, except for a handkerchief, a paperclip, and a chocolate bar. "How about sharing this chocolate bar?" Alice proposed. "That way, you have gained something from our meeting, but as I share it with you freely, it does not count as robbing."

The Triggerfish smiled with delight. "An excellent suggestion!"

And so she broke the chocolate bar in two and gave one part to the Triggerfish, while she happily munched on the other. After they both had finished their share, they just faced each other in silence for a time. The Triggerfish was obviously growing quite uncomfortable with the situation. Apparently feeling it was his job to do something piraty now, it blew up its chest to make itself look like it was completely in control, and said to Alice in a voice that hardly hid its nervousness: "Arrr, well, I suppose that's it then! There is nothing more I want of you, so I declare you're free to go now. Be off, before I make you walk the plank!"

Alice tried not to smile and said politely: "It was very nice meeting you. And thank you for not robbing me!" Then she turned and walked away. In the distance she could still hear the Triggerfish shout to no one in particular: "Ahoy, you scurvy dogs! Bring a spring upon 'er and swab the decks! Heave ho, or I'll have you flogged!"

For the first minute or two the path went straight on, but then, after following a bend in the road, she found herself facing a crossing. "This must be the crossing the Saw-Shark was referring to," she thought. But what a strange crossing it was! Instead of the path splitting up into one or two side roads, it split into a multitude of paths that doubled up on themselves, went in circles, or crossed other paths several times. Also there were bridges and tunnels that made paths to go over or under other paths. "I would call this a *maze* instead of a crossing," muttered Alice, "as it does not resemble a cross at all. Why, some of these roads look more like corkscrews that keep intersecting with themselves! How am I supposed to know which path to take?"

Alice stood looking at the crossing several minutes, trying to figure out which path led to where. "Let's see, the Saw-Shark told me to make a left turn and take routes 4 and 16. But there is no route with any of those numbers! And did he mean I should take the first path that rotates to the left, or that I should take the path that *actually* takes me to the left? For as far as I can see, the path turning to the left will lead right to the opposite side!" But alas, there was no one here to ask. "Seeing how they were building that house, I might not be able to trust their directions *at all*," Alice complained.

After some sighing, some head rubbing, and some stomping her foot to the ground in frustration (none of which helped), she finally decided to try the actual left. "I'll pay really close attention to where I'm going, so I can always track back to this crossing and take one of the other paths, when it turns out that this was the wrong way. This strange rock should be a good first landmark to remember!" (Alice was very glad she could recall these instructions from her parents. They had come in handy several times before already, as she had a tendency to wander off to explore strange new places, but did not like the thought of getting lost and missing a meal.) And bravely she went on, again trying to keep quiet.

The path continued for quite a while, without any more crossings. After having walked for about ten minutes, Alice got the feeling she was starting to walk uphill. "I do think the lake is getting more shallow here. Could I be reaching the other end of it? Perhaps I did take the wrong path then, as I still have not found the Queen Bee's court!"

What made things harder, was that it was getting more and more difficult to see where she was walking, as it appeared to grow darker each minute. "It ca'n't be evening already," wondered Alice: "I have not been down here *that* long, I'm sure!" She quickly checked her skin, to see how much it had begun wrinkling by now. But it was as smooth as ever. Still, there was no denying that it *was* getting dark. "Perhaps the Tuna has somehow managed to move the sun or moon already," she thought. "But no, bamboo cannot grow so very quickly, I'm sure of that as well!" Still, the light was fading rapidly.

Alice then became aware of a tall shadow floating in overhead. It was so large that it was covering almost all of the visible waterline above her. "Oh dear! The Scuttleflot!" she realised in horror. Alice tried to turn around and run, but it was too late. There was a splash, and then a large, monstrous head appeared in front of her.

The head was attached to the longest neck Alice had ever seen, which went all the way up towards the dark shadow, which she assumed was the Scuttleflot's body—or boat. "I must flee right now!" thought Alice, but no part of her body was willing to obey her anymore. She could only stand in the same spot, looking at the Scuttleflot, completely frozen.

"Why, hello there," said the Scuttleflot. Its voice sounded like a warm humming, with a little rumble in the back. "Like a hot summer day, when you can hear a thunderstorm approach," thought Alice.

"Aren't you going to say something? Has your tongue got the cat?" asked the Scuttleflot, and rumbled softly.

"I—why—no!" stammered Alice. "You're confusing me!"

"Why?" murmured the Scuttleflot.

"Well—for one, you haven't begun eating me yet. And then, you swapped the expression 'has the cat got your tongue'," Alice blurted out, surprised she was having this conversation at all.

"I did not," said the Scuttleflot with a slight grin, that showed Alice a glimpse of its huge teeth. "'Cat got your tongue' is obviously nonsense. How should it be able to get it? You'd have to be extremely careless. Are you a careless girl?" it asked, and tilted its head provocatively.

"No, I'm not," said Alice timidly, "but isn't the other way around nonsense as well? How can a tongue get a cat?"

Instead of answering her question, the Scuttleflot opened its mouth and let a large, very thin tongue slide out. Alice thought it

looked like the tongue of a salamander. The tongue kept protruding further and further, until the end reached about fifteen feet past Alice, where it curled around an unsuspecting fish as a snake would curl around its prey. Only when the Scuttleflot retracted its tongue again did it begin to speak. "Lhee? And it'lh vewwy harg ko lhkeak wheng youe koung haj lhonglhing!"

"I beg your pardon, I have no idea what you're trying to say," trembled Alice, trying to suppress a nervous scream of laughter.

The Scuttleflot's tongue had by now completely retracted into its mouth, taking the poor fish with it. The Scuttleflot swallowed and spoke again in its soft, controlled voice, which Alice actually found far more frightening than if it had bellowed at her. "I was demonstrating that it's very hard to speak when your tongue has got something. So you see, the expression does make more sense my way," it said.

"Indeed, when you have a tongue a long as yours!" admitted Alice. She wisely left out that she could actually very well picture Dinah catching such a tongue, as it resembled a piece of yarn, and Dinah *loved* chasing and catching yarn.

"So then, now that we've got this out of the way—let's head on to your other remark," said the Scuttleflot. "Why would you think I'd eat you?"

Alice thought that was very obvious. "Why, because monsters eat people! That is well known!"

"I see, you think you know everything," said the Scuttleflot. "Perhaps you are an expert on monsters? How many have you met before?"

"You're the first one, to be honest," admitted Alice. "Actually, I make it a point to stay out of their way."

"Now *that* is the first wise thing you have said until now," grinned the Scuttleflot. "But you still have a lot to learn. For one, I am a pescaterian. That means I don't eat meat, only plants and seafood, you see."

Alice looked at the Scuttleflot suspiciously.

"You don't trust me?" it asked, and grinning even more widely, it added: "I'm actually quite agreeable, would you believe that? I would even say—*benign.*"

As soon as the Scuttleflot had spoken, there was a loud BANG! somewhere above their heads.

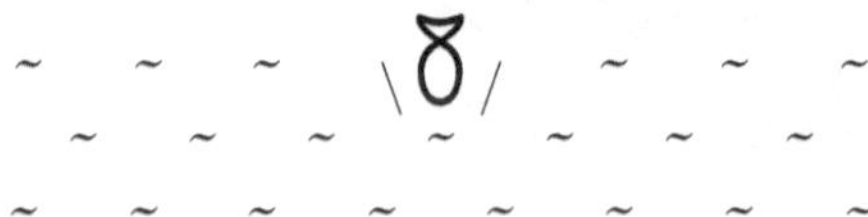

It startled Alice greatly, but the Scuttleflot looked only very much amused and continued, while keeping its dark eyes fixated on her: "That is—unless I get *very* hungry of course. And after all, you

100

being under water now *does* make you seafood, by definition, I would say." Its stomach growled dangerously.

"I wo'n't be eaten!" shouted Alice defiantly.

Suddenly, several things started happening all at once. Shouting seemed to make Alice's courage reappear—her limbs began cooperating in response and she was finally able to turn around and run, which she did immediately. At the same time, a shell rose up from the sand and hit the Scuttleflot from underneath. It howled in pain, and there was a very bright light, which blinded Alice. Although she couldn't see a single thing anymore, she did not wait for either her eyes or the Scuttleflot to recover: she ran as fast as her legs could carry her, desperately hoping that she would not run into anything.

CHAPTER IX

A Traffic Jam

ALICE ran until she could no longer hear the howling of the Scuttleflot, and then some more. Luckily, she had only brushed a couple of soft plants during her flight and until now had somehow managed to keep her footing every time she stumbled on a rock. "That *was* a narrow escape," she was just thinking to herself, when alas!—her foot got caught on a big rock and *thump!*—down towards the ground she went!

As she lay panting on the sand, Alice wondered how long it would take to get her vision back, if at all, as she was still not able to see a single thing. She blinked her eyes several times, but everything around her remained pitch black. Which made her startle only more, when a languid and hollow voice sounded close behind her.

"Are—you—all—right?"

Alice found she could hardly speak yet. "Yes—but I—need to—catch my breath!" she gasped.

"Then—don't—stop—running—otherwise—it—will—*certainly*—get—away," the voice spoke.

Although the voice sounded friendly, Alice realised that she had no idea whom she was speaking to, and, judging by her most recent encounters, it might just be anything. Before sitting up, she started feeling around, to see if she could find the creature.

"Ouch!" it exclaimed, when her foot accidentally hit something again. "Stop—scrambling—around! You'll—poke—some—one's—eye—out!"

"I'm truly sorry," said Alice, who was finally able to control her breathing, "I just don't want to accidentally sit down on you."

"Sitting—down—on—some—one—on—purpose—is—not—very—nice—either," the voice remarked indignantly.

"That's not what I mean to say," protested Alice.

"Nevertheless—what—you—say—is—too—mean," it said in rebuke. "Seems—to—me—that—your—mouth—hasn't—yet—stopped—running."

Alice decided to ignore its last comment. After she had made sure there was nothing in the way, she sat up and made herself comfortable on the sandy floor. She then noticed a tiny light in the distance, which seemed to be coming nearer. "Which is a strange thing to see when you're blinded," Alice thought to herself, rather puzzled. "Maybe I hit my head on the ground when I fell, and am now hearing voices and seeing things that are not really here!" She tried closing and opening her eyes several times, but the light seemed to be as real as the voice had appeared to be. It kept getting nearer, until she could make out what it was. The little light turned out to dangle from an antenna, which was attached to the head of a *very* ugly fish. Not only was it ugly, it also had a *huge* mouth with even bigger teeth! Alice began to scramble up, preparing herself to bolt once more, when the sluggish voice said: "No—worries—she's—friendly."

Alice wasn't at all sure about that, but also wasn't looking forward to running in the dark again, without any idea where she was going, and as the creature was approaching quite slowly, not looking as if she wanted to attack her, Alice decided to take her chances and stay put.

Once the Anglerfish had got close enough for her to speak to, Alice was also finally able to see her surroundings. She found herself in a medium sized cave. "Which explains why I wasn't able to see anything," she realised. "The walls are blocking the light! I must accidentally have run into an opening while fleeing from the Scuttleflot." She now also discovered what had produced the voice. The rock she had stumbled on wasn't a rock at all—it was a turtle! And it was lying on its back, its paws wiggling in vain to all sides. She quickly picked it up and set it upright again.

Much to Alice's relief, the Anglerfish did nothing but stare at them and yawn. After an uncomfortable silence, Alice decided to begin a conversation. "Thank you for lighting up the place," Alice said to her. "It's so nice to be able to see again after all this darkness!"

"What darkness?" sighed the Anglerfish. "There is no darkness in this lake. Not to the right, not to the left, not in front of me—not anywhere! *Ever!*" And she yawned again.

"I suppose you'll never have to be afraid of the dark with that light of yours," Alice went on. "It must very much come in handy when you're trying to sleep and hear scary noises, or when you think there's something underneath your bed."

"I wish I were able to sleep!" complained the Anglerfish. "How can I, when there's always such a bright light in front of my eyes!"

"Ca'n't you turn it off?" asked Alice.

"No, that's the problem!" the Anglerfish said. "It's always on. I've tried everything I could think of: hitting it with a club, switching all my buttons, not paying my electric bill—I've even persuaded my friend to invite it to a ball. But it's no use—it wo'n't go out. And I'm *so* tired. Please, ca'n't you help me get some sleep?"

Alice considered. "Well, I could sing you a lullaby. Would that help?"

"I don't know," said the Anglerfish. "Would you be willing to try?"

"Sure," said Alice, and cleared her throat. But of course, the song again came out all different than the way she had learned it:—

> *"Hush little fishy, don't stay awake,*
> *Mama's gonna buy you a rattlesnake.*
>
> *And if that rattlesnake wo'n't bite,*
> *Mama's gonna make its tail ignite.*
>
> *And if that fire wo'n't be hot,*
> *Mama's gonna tie it in a knot.*
>
> *And if that knot can be undone,*
> *Mama's gonna get the biggest gun.*
>
> *And if that gun wo'n't shoot it dead,*
> *Mama's gonna stomp its head instead.*
>
> *And if its head cannot be crushed,*
> *Mama's gonna get its body flushed.*
>
> *And if it makes the toilet clog,*
> *Mama's gonna feed it all her grog.*

And if the grog wo'n't make it sick,
Mama's gonna give it a giant kick.

And if that kick wo'n't make it disappear,
You'll still be the sleepiest little fish down here!"

"That's horrible!" exclaimed the Anglerfish.

"I'm so sorry!" cried Alice, "That's not at all what I wanted to sing! I think I'm still shaken up by my encounter with the Scuttleflot."

"And—how—exactly—will—a—rattlesnake—help—you—sleep?" asked the Turtle.

Alice thought it better not to answer that. "Perhaps we should try something else."

The three of them sat in silence for several minutes, thinking about how to solve this problem. After a time, Alice remembered the handkerchief in her pocket. She took it out and said: "Here, let's try this!" She folded the handkerchief in two, placed it over the light and tied the ends in a knot around it. And behold—there was darkness again!

"Thank you so much!" the Anglerfish rejoiced. "I'll finally be able to sleep now! I'm going to seek out my bed immediately!" And she swam away in a hurry, leaving Alice and the Turtle alone in the dark again. Judging by the amount of *ouch*es and *oof*s they heard, she kept swimming into the cave walls while making her way out, but the sounds kept getting fainter until at last neither of them was able to hear her anymore.

"Well, I suppose she's pleased now," she said. (Although Alice thought she herself might now not ever be able to sleep again, as both the images of the Scuttleflot and this creepy fish had firmly settled into her mind.) "But how am *I* now going to find my way out of this cave?"

"Just—follow—the—walls," the Turtle advised. "There's—only—one—tunnel."

"I will do that, thank you," said Alice. She got up and searched for one of the walls. It didn't take her long to find one—it felt cold and rough to her touch. Alice then began walking while making sure her hand kept touching the wall. Indeed, after about only a minute, she saw a bright light marking the end of the cave.

Alice held her hands before her eyes to shield them from the light, which was now much too bright for her, after having been in the dark for so long. She decided to stay where she was until her eyes had grown used to the light again. After a minute or so, she was finally able to see her surroundings. To her right, she distinguished a long line of tightly packed creatures floating in the water. More kept arriving from the left, adding themselves to the queue.

"What's going on?" shouted one of the newly arrived fish to the creatures further in line.

"Don't know!" one of them shouted back. "Hey you, over there," it said to those even further along in the queue, "What's going on?"

And Alice could hear the question being repeated throughout the line of fishes, like a fading echo. After a while, the answer returned in the form of another echo message: "There's a zebra crossing beyond! It's having trouble reaching the other side of the road because the water is so hard over there!"

The face of the fish at the end lighted up. "You all know what that means, right?"

And then the whole queue cried out as one: "TRAFFIC JAM!"

All of a sudden all the fish were holding instruments and began playing them as loudly as they could. (Alice had no idea where they got the instruments from, as the creatures had no pockets and hadn't been carrying any bags. Even if they had, most instruments were far too large to have been stuffed in there anyway.) One fish was strumming a ukulele, and another one appeared to be playing a xylophone—which it had strapped to its body to keep it from sinking. Further on there were three blue fish blowing on shells

108

shaped like horns, and another had a didgeridoo made out of a piece of bamboo. Others had resorted to using their fellow queuers to produce sounds: one was strumming the barbels of a catfish, the shell of a turtle served as a drum, and mussels were being used as castanets. A blowfish and a bass were playing themselves—the blowfish had stuck several pieces of reed into itself and now functioned as a bagpipe. Unfortunately, and contrary to their earlier unified cry, they apparently did *not* agree about what they would be playing, as everyone had picked a tune of their own choice. To make matters worse, they were all in a different tempo and rhythm, and of course each had their own scales as well.

As new fish kept arriving and joining in with the musical cacophony, it very soon became rather crowded. Alice had to press her back to the cave wall in order not to be assimilated into the queue. She also had to duck aside several times to avoid the bow of a violin poking her eye out, while at the same time being careful not to get in the way of the slide of a trombone. Even with her hands pressed against her ears, the noise was becoming unbearable. "You're too much off pitch!" she exclaimed in a desperate voice.

"Pitch!" one of the fishes shouted.

"Pitch!" several others repeated. More and more fish kept picking up the cry, until all who did not need their mouths to play their instruments were chanting it simultaneously. At the same time, they were starting to move in the water—up and down, up and down—but with a little delay relative to the fish in front of them. Soon they had created a movement resembling a sine wave (you know, just like the audiences of football matches sometimes make when they are cheering for the players). The wave became higher and higher, which had quite an effect on the water. A strong current was forming and Alice had to grab hold of the cave wall to prevent being swept off her feet. But the fish kept making larger and larger waves and finally there was no more to be done about it: her fingers could no longer keep hold and the current carried her away at high speed.

At first Alice tried to resist by swimming against it, but not only was it *very* fatiguing, it also made no difference whatsoever. "I might as well succumb to it," she thought. "After all, I had no idea where I was or which way I should be heading anyway, so this direction is as good as any."

CHAPTER X

Dumpster Diving

THE current led Alice past many grounds, much more quickly than she would have been able to cross on foot. She had plenty of time to look around, and noticed that other creatures were taking advantage of the current as well: she passed a couple of mackerels that were flying kites in the stream (which made Alice wonder why it was not called "floating kites", as she thought this expression would actually be much more befitting for both the activity under *and* above water), and little creatures kept joining her to float along for a while. Among others, she was briefly accompanied by a couple of shrimps who were cheering about this newly created highway, but after a few minutes they broke loose of the stream and swam on in their desired direction, leaving Alice all by herself again. Not only did inhabitants of the lake join her—objects were dragged into the stream as well. On closer inspection, she discovered the objects were pieces of rubbish and discarded items.

Finally the current began to lose its strength, and she slowly drifted down to the bottom of the lake. The rubbish first kept fluttering around her for a while, but eventually the smaller pieces went up to the lake's surface, where they floated around in circles. The larger pieces of litter sunk to the bottom and joined the heaps of rubbish which had apparently been gathering there for quite some time. "Some one ought to clean this up," Alice muttered.

Among the rubbish was a yellow rubber ducky. Alice picked it up and wiped some smudges off it. "Why would any one discard you?" she asked it. To be honest, by now she had become so used to sea creatures and inanimate objects speaking to her, that she was actually surprised when it *didn't* respond. A bit disappointed, she put it back on the heap.

After inspecting her surroundings, in the hopes of finding some clue as to her current whereabouts, Alice noticed that there were little strings of tiny balls attached to almost every plant around her. "Fish eggs!" she exclaimed. "Why, this seems to be some sort of breeding area." She got up to study them more closely, but when she scrambled over the piles of rubbish to reach them, her foot got stuck, and no matter how much she wriggled to get it out, it was no use. With a sigh, she sat down on another discarded item (which looked as though it had once been a storage box), and put her head in her hands.

"What a mess," she said to the ducky in a melancholy voice. (Even though it could not understand her, she felt it was better than talking to nobody at all.) "Here I am, somewhere at the bottom of a lake, with neither an idea where I am, nor which way I should go. Even if I decided to give up trying to meet the Queen Bee, I'd have no idea in which direction I should be heading to get back to our boat. And if I *did* know where to go, I couldn't go, because I'm stuck!"

Her self-pity did not last long—two cormorants that seemed to be in an even more miserable position than Alice were drifting towards the heap of rubbish. The poor birds had got their heads completely entangled in a piece of packaging material. Alice wasn't sure what was annoying them most: being stuck in litter, or being stuck in the same piece together, as they were arguing with each other quite loudly.

"I told you we should not swim this way," said one of them. "Look where we ended up!"

"And *I* told *you* to shut your beak," said the other. "Your whining is enough to make a turtle move house!"

"At least *I* am trying to find a solution, which is more than you have ever done since you were born!" his fellow Cormorant rebuked.

"Don't make me laugh! Bossing me around is the only thing you have done so far!" said the other. "Find some one else to do your biddings, 'cause *I* am tired of it!"

The first Cormorant angrily looked away from its companion, but then something on the lake bottom caught its eye and it shouted: "Hey, you—poolboy! Help us get out of this, will you?"

Surprised, Alice looked in the direction it had shouted. Only then she noticed the *very* strange creature that was scrambling around something resembling a buoy, and gathering waste with a litter picker. She was not sure what it was, not even if it was a fish. Regardless of its strangeness, it was also looking *extremely* cute. It was pink, and although its body had the shape of a fish, with a tail like that of an eel, it also had four paws sticking out of its sides. On each side of its head, which was broad and wide and contained a wide mouth, were three protrusions, which resembled tentacles—or plants, Alice couldn't say for sure. "How fun it would be to have this creature as a pet!" she thought to herself. "I could look at it all day! But then again, how would Dinah feel about it? She *is* very fond of fish, but perhaps not in the right way."

The creature looked up with an offended look in its eyes after it heard the Cormorant call. "Who are you calling 'poolboy'? I'm the guardian of these grounds! The protector of the plug!"

"Yes of course, and the defender of debris, by the looks of it," the second Cormorant mocked.

"I ca'n't help it," sulked the strange creature. "There is so much rubbish here, I have to clean it up to be able to do my job! All thanks to people—like *her*!" It pointed to Alice.

"*I* didn't throw all this away!" Alice objected.

"You're human, are you not?" said the creature.

"Yes," admitted Alice, "but I separate my waste."

"What's the use of that," cried one of the Cormorants, "if you throw it all away anyway? You better come up and separate *us*!"

"I would if I could," said Alice, "but I'm stuck myself, you see." She turned to the strange creature. "Could you please help me,

Sir—or Ma'am—" she hesitated: "I'm sorry, but what *are* you, if I may be so bold to ask? I've never seen anything like you!"

"I'm an axolotl," it replied. "Here, let me get you out of this. Because *you* asked *nicely*," it added, looking up to the Cormorants reproachfully.

Once Alice was freed she got up, stood on her toes, and reached out to the floating birds. She grabbed one of them by the paw in order to pull them towards her. This however was met with great

114

protest and struggle. "Do you want me to set you free or not?" Alice asked in an irritated voice, after she had been kicked in the face two times by the birds. They then let her pull them down, but getting them free from the material they had got themselves stuck into was a whole different challenge. They kept flapping their wings and squeaking loudly. "Hold still!" she cried. "How can I ever get your heads through this when you keep spreading your beaks wide open!" Eventually she had to clamp their beaks shut with her hand one by one, then sit on it, then try to squeeze their heads out of the packaging with both her hands, and then quickly get up to pull the opening over their beaks before they had time to open them again. After a struggle of several minutes, she finally managed to get them both loose.

"Come, now that we are all freed from the litter, we can have a proper conversation," thought Alice. "Would you tell me, Sir, what you're supposed to be doing here, if it isn't cleaning up rubbish?"

The Axolotl sighed. "I'm actually here to guard the plug. But I ca'n't keep an eye on it properly if it keeps getting covered in rubbish!"

"What plug?" Alice asked in a surprised voice.

"Why, that one, of course," the Axolotl replied, and pointed to the thing it had been crawling next to when she first noticed it. And indeed, when she looked closer, Alice discovered that what she had mistaken for a buoy, was actually a large plug, tightly fastened in the ground.

"Why is there a plug in the ground?" Alice exclaimed.

"To prevent the lake from draining. I'd say that is quite obvious. How'd you think we make all the water stay up here?"

Alice had to admit she had never given it a thought before.

"This is the most important place in the whole lake," the Axolotl continued. "It's the place where everything begins, and also where everything ends."

Alice began to worry. "I hope this does not apply to *me*! I didn't start here, and I'd rather not be finished here either."

The Axolotl frowned. "Don't you like my company? I am
actually a very pleasant companion, if I may say so myself. Here, let
me entertain you all by reciting a poem!" And before Alice or the
Cormorants could say anything, it began:—

> *"There once had been a conger eel*
>   *Who struggled to confess —*
> *He never had a fashion sense*
>   *And loved to overdress.*
> *His friends told him to tone it down*
>   *Yet he wore nothing less.*
>
> *But when he swam outside one day*
>   *The other fishes cried:*
> *"You look just like a butternut!" —*
>   *Which made him want to hide.*
> *He fled into his house to wait*
>   *Until his tears had dried.*
>
> *But soon he had his mind made up*
>   *That he would not give in —*
> *He'd rather face lobotomy,*
>   *Or strain his dorsal fin,*
> *Than hide into oblivion,*
>   *And live life as in sin.*
>
> *He asked a tailor to stop by,*
>   *And make a work of art;*
> *Outrageous and extravagant*
>   *So lips would spread apart!*
> *"Do sew a sea cucumber in,"*
>   *He hinted as a start.*

The tailor said: "It ca'n't be done;
This is preposterous!
This order is beyond my skill,"
And ran under a bus —
While holding nitroglycerin —
Which caused tremendous fuss.

"I will not quit," resolved the eel.
"I sha'n't abandon hope."
He took a pen and wrote his wishes
On a bar of soap.
Then sent it to an artist in
A window envelope.

The artist came as soon as he
Had read the eel's request.
He took the job that was at hand,
And clearly he expressed
The garment which he had in mind
To make him look his best.

Three days later it was done;
The eel had no complaint.
He flaunted proudly through the streets
Without any restraint;
Completely naked and instead
Adorned with body paint!"

"That was very entertaining indeed!" smiled Alice, after the Axolotl had finished. "But I'm afraid you misunderstood me. I didn't mean you are bad company, I just want to get back home—which is not in this lake. Preferably *after* I have spoken to the Queen Bee. But I have no idea where I am at the moment."

"Then you're in luck," said the Axolotl, "because I happen to know *exactly* where we are."

"Yeah, so do we," said one of the Cormorants. "At the bottom of a lake!"

"Great!" said Alice, ignoring the Cormorant and feeling very much relieved. "Then which way should I go from here?"

"I haven't got the slightest idea," said the Axolotl. "That's a completely different question, obviously. You don't need to know where you are in order to determine where you should be heading to."

"Well, I know where I want to go, I just don't know how to get there," Alice clarified.

The Axolotl looked at her very earnestly. "If you want my advice: when I want to go forward, I never take the road that lead me to where I am now."

That sounded like good advice to Alice, but it did not actually help her current situation. "Oh, how I wish to see my sisters again," she said in a very melancholy voice. "I never thought I would miss them so much!"

"There is a tale about sisters connected to this plug, you know," said the Axolotl. "Would you like to hear it?"

"Yes, please," said Alice, who hoped the story would be comforting, and made herself a bit more comfy on the heap of litter. The Cormorants tried to look uninterested, but moved in closer nevertheless.

"There once were three sisters," the Axolotl began: "Corvina, who was named after her mother, Allie, the alligator, and Tillie, the tilapia. They were playing hide and seek in this area. Corvina insisted on being the seeker, because she was the oldest and therefore claimed to be the best at counting—"

"Oldest siblings always are know-it-alls, aren't they?" interrupted Alice.

"They are not!" said the largest Cormorant, a little offended. "And I would know. *I* am the oldest among *my* siblings."

The other Cormorant made a face behind its back.

"Anyway," the Axolotl continued, "Tillie objected that the game wasn't fair, as she had more trouble hiding than Allie, but her sisters ignored her complaints. So Allie and Tillie then looked for places to hide.

This time it was the smaller Cormorant that interrupted the story. "Why did Tillie have more trouble hiding? A tilapia is much smaller than an alligator, so it should be easier for her!"

"Yes, but alligators can leave the water. So they have more places to hide," answered the Axolotl.

"But that wouldn't be fair to Corvina," Alice objected. "She ca'n't leave the water either, so she would never be able to find Allie."

"Which is the point of the game, isn't it?" asked the Axolotl. "Now, do you want to hear the story or not?"

When Alice and the Cormorants kept silent, it continued: "Little Tillie discovered the plug and thought it would be a good place to hide under. So she lifted the plug, but then a strong current pulled her *right* into the hole, and then pulled the plug securely back on."

The beak of the largest Cormorant fell open, but the smaller one immediately clasped it shut.

"Her sisters did not see Tillie again after that. And ever since, the plug has never again been lifted. It is being guarded now to prevent other fish from suffering the same fate."

"Poor Tillie!" Alice cried out.

"Yes, but it is said that this was not the end of her," the Axolotl added in a hushed voice. "You see, no one knows where the hole leads to. There is a prophecy that Tillie has ended up in another place, and will one day find her way back here to dethrone the Queen Bee."

"I would very much like to believe that," Alice said, when a piece of cloth floated into her face. She pulled it off and looked at it in disgust. "What is this?"

"Just more litter," the Axolotl responded with a sigh. "I think the plug may be leaking a little, causing a slight current that leads all debris in the lake right here."

Alice got up from the pile of rubbish she was sitting on and decided to follow the debris to its origin, as more rags were floating in. The further on she went, the more pieces there were in the water. She began gathering the rags that floated past her while walking, and she already had a whole arm full when she found the source of the debris: it was two fish busily ripping up a large pile of ties. To her surprise, one of them was the red herring that had startled her at the lake shore earlier that day.

"You're not making the pieces small enough!" the Red Herring was just complaining to the other fish. "Stop cutting corners!"

"I am doing my share! I already did so much this morning, when I was here all by myself!" his workfellow objected.

"You definitely did far too little of much," countered the Red Herring. "I bet you were stuffing yourself with bread and butter again, weren't you?"

"It was only bread—you used up all the butter, remember?" the other one muttered.

Both fish were so focused on their argument, that they didn't notice Alice until she was standing right next to them. Once they did, they each made a back somersault from fright and then looked at her with their mouths hanging open. Alice thought that made them look incredibly stupid and she had to make an effort not to laugh.

"Oh please," she said, "close your mouths, you silly fish!"

"I'm not a silly fish," said the Red Herring. "I'm a herring. And this—" pointing to the other fish, "—is a haddock."

"Nice to meet you. My name is Alice," she said in response. "May I ask what you are doing? You're making quite a mess, you know."

"We're destroying all ties!" said the Haddock.

"By order of the Queen!" confirmed the Red Herring.

"I can see that. But why would she want you to destroy *ties*?" Alice asked in astonishment.

"Because they are from overseas," said the Haddock. "They cost us way too much, you see."

"And we don't like their colours either," the Red Herring chimed in. "Better to get rid of them. Before you know it, them from over there are taking over all our jobs."

"Yes," said the Haddock, "and we can do a much better job ourselves!"

"I'm sure you can make your own," said Alice, "but I don't really see any need to destroy the ties you already have at the moment. If you have to remake them all again yourself, wouldn't that cost you more than if you'd just keep these?"

"Yeah, we realise that now. But we all voted for it," said the Haddock.

"Well, ca'n't you change your minds?" asked Alice.

"Certainly not—it's the principle that counts! We tried negotiating with them, but they were very stubborn! It's their fault that we are not buying anything from them anymore!"

"Indeed it is!" the Red Herring cried. "We made them a very good offer: we would allow them to keep delivering their wares to us for free! But they refused. Can you believe it?"

Alice looked puzzled. "Actually, I can. I don't see why they should keep giving you things, if you no longer give anything back."

"Either way, it's no use telling *us*. We'll have to do this now, whether we like it or not," said the Haddock.

"Court-ordered community service," sighed the Red Herring. "They found me to be too distracting to others."

"Why?" asked Alice. "What did you do?"

"It was nothing, really. While the Queen Bee was having tea, I merely remarked: 'Watch out, the Scuttleflot!' It wasn't *my* fault that everyone then panicked and knocked over her throne while trying to get away, was it?"

Both the Red Herring and the Haddock smirked.

"Perhaps it wasn't a very clever thing to do, but it does not sound like a crime to me," said Alice. She turned to the Haddock. "What did you do to get punished?" she asked. "If you don't mind me asking, that is."

"Nothing at all! I was only defending myself," he said. "They were hunting me for my eyes, you see."

"That seems quite unfair as well," concluded Alice. "I don't think the court's ruling is very sound."

"And their punishments aren't very light, either! But *I* am not about to complain about that, I assure you!" said the Red Herring. "Before you know, they'll hang us!"

"The trick is to not get caught," said the Haddock. "Some of us are easier to catch than others, apparently. For example, have you ever caught a crab?"

"No, but I did catch a cold several times," Alice replied.

"So you don't know how to catch crabs? Take a guess!" said the Haddock.

Alice considered. "Well, I heard my aunt was able to beat her cancer because it was caught early, so—I suppose you can do it with a stick in the mornings?"

"Dear me, no! You shouldn't beat them!" said the Haddock, disapprovingly.

"Then what should I do?" asked Alice.

"If you ca'n't beat them, join them!" exclaimed the Red Herring. "You should tie 'em up on a string."

"It's called crab lining," explained the Haddock. "But you'll need to use a catch phrase first. You see, you have to—"

Their conversation got rudely interrupted by the sound of a horn blowing. "It's the Queen's trumpeter!" said the Red Herring after having looked over its shoulder.

The Trumpeter sounded his horn several times again, then took a deep breath and exclaimed:—

> *"All present here, take heed of me:*
>   *There'll be a party, free for all!*
> *The best of parties it will be!*
>   *This fête behind our wall.*
>   *We'll make the empire eat again,*
>   *And I will tell you where and when.*
>
> *You are invited by the Queen,*
>   *And we will serve the finest cake.*
> *The greatest you have ever seen!*
>   *This news sure isn't fake!*
>   *Let's heat the waters up to-day —*
>   *It is too cold here anyway.*

Covfefe! Soon the feast will start!
So grab your women and their cats!
Put in my greatest friend, so smart!
You're welcome! See, and that's
so big a tree, seats any guest;
As host I surely am the best!"

He looked around, boastfully, to see if any one was paying attention. Apparently he thought he didn't get any, or at least, not enough, so in an even louder voice he continued:—

"Yesterday they said I'm peach—meant:
I am orange—they are so wrong!
And I don't need their full consent
To sing my excellent song!
I'll send it with a tweety bird;
I'll do it, probably, maybe definitely."

And then all of a sudden he left off, turned around and swam away angrily, leaving Alice, the Haddock and the Red Herring completely bewildered.

"His poetry is even worse than the Goby's," Alice thought to herself. To the others, she said: "Is it just me, or is his message dreadfully confusing? And I'm not at all sure his sentences are grammatically correct. Also, that last line didn't fit the metre, or even rhyme!"

"He always does that," said the Haddock. "He doesn't care about his phrasing, as long as he can blow his trumpet. The problem is, what he says or does makes no difference at all to the crowds; they listen to him anyway."

"Well, I can imagine they do, if he promises them a free party!" said Alice, not noticing a soft splashing far away—

—and then asked hopefully: "Would they mind another attendee?" (Alice did not want to crash a party in some one else's empire, but was also not willing to forego cake if she could help it.)

"Not at all. Come on!" shouted the Haddock, ignoring the shell that was making its way up toward the lake's surface. Alice and the Red Herring joined with him and quickly made their way to the court.

CHAPTER XI

The Queen's Court

IT did not take them long to get there. Before Alice knew it, a beautiful castle loomed up, surrounded by extremely well-kept gardens that housed corals in more gorgeous colours than she could count. Meandering paths lined with colourful pebbles crossed the gardens. Here and there were fountains, placed throughout the courtyard in symmetrical patterns. Instead of water, they were sprouting bubbles of air. Colourful garlands were put up, and to top it all off, electric eels were sparking above the crowds. (Which, Alice assumed, was probably the under-water alternative to fireworks.)

"I finally made it!" Alice cheered to herself. "Now I'll be able to see the Queen Bee. Surely there must be a moment during the party that I can speak to her?"

Quite a number of guests had gathered in the gardens and the party seemed to have started already. It looked as if the guests were amusing themselves very well. There were gouramis surfing the fountains on plates they had acquired from the party tables. Guppies were playing tennis, using their tails as rackets. And a cast of crabs was playing a game that Alice thought must be some version of football. However, as the crabs were only able to walk sideways, they had lined up in rows and the game progressed quite like a table football match, in which a whole line would start shifting to one side to block the ball when it came their way, after which another line of players would start moving sideways when the ball happened to pass through. Once Alice saw the ball make it all the way to the goalkeeper. It easily snatched up the ball in its claws, though immediately thereafter a loud pop! was heard. Sounds of

disappointment emerged from both teams of crab players, mixed with exclamations of "not *again!*"

Alice looked over to the party tables. They were covered with food, some of it looking quite delicious to her, some not at all. A marlin was serving skewered vegetables from its bill, but most guests were helping themselves. A tetra was busy chewing itself right through one of the larger cakes, and a pelican was stuffing its pouch full with anything it could get its wings on. Alice also noticed one fish chasing another, much smaller, guest in an attempt to eat it. The poor little fish only got away because its assailant had to flee itself before the hungry mouth of an even bigger guest. "One would think they'd have rules here about not eating other guests," Alice said disapprovingly. But no one seemed to mind. The Haddock, who was standing next to her, also merely shrugged his shoulders.

"I shouldn't mind something to eat or drink, myself," remarked Alice, who remembered that she still hadn't had anything since her arrival in the lake, except for the piece of chocolate bar. "The service is terrible—we've been standing here for quite some time, and none of the waiters has offered us anything!"

"Of course not!" replied the Haddock. "What did you expect? They are waiters—they are waiting for *you* to call *them!*"

Alice thought that there was some sense in this, and decided to keep it in mind for the next time her father complained about the restaurant staff taking too long to bring their order. Without hesitating, she made eye contact with the waiter swimming nearest to them, which was a hamlet fish. It immediately swam up to them and offered Alice and the others a drink from its tray, which came in a cup with a lid and straw. She examined it closely and then carefully took a sip. She was not at all disappointed about the taste, which was very, very sweet. "What is it?" she asked.

"It's honey mead. Specially brewed for our Queen!"

"It's very good!"

"There is nothing either good or bad, but drinking makes it so," responded the Waiter.

"If you say so," said Alice. The thought came to her mind that she might be able to get in touch with the Queen through one of her employees, and so it might be wise to engage this one in a conversation. "My name is Alice. May I ask you a question? As you work here, do you happen to know Goby, the former court jester? I met him on my way here."

"Ah yes," the Waiter sighed. "Alas, poor Goby! I knew him, Alice. A fish of infinite jest, of most excellent fancy. Where be your gyres now? Your gimbles? Your songs?"

"I know," said Alice. "It's very unfortunate that he was sent away. He told me he is not at all happy in his new job."

"That Goby doth protest too much, methinks," said the Waiter. "He should be lucky the Queen has merely relocated him. Some are born bait, some achieve lameness, and some have graveness thrust upon them!"

"I'm glad that didn't happen to him," said Alice "but still, it is unfortunate that he wasn't allowed to be the court jester anymore. Say, I would really like to speak with the Queen Bee. Do you suppose there is a way for me to get to see her?"

"To see, or not to see—that is the question?" asked the Waiter.

"Well, yes, you could put it that way," said Alice, hesitating. "Perhaps you can announce my arrival to her? You can tell her I'm here to speak about the sinking of my boat."

"Shall I compare thee to a castaway?" the Waiter suggested.

"No, that wo'n't do at all!" said Alice impatiently. She was becoming frustrated by the conversation and the Waiter not seeming to understand her. "I only want you to arrange an opportunity for me to talk to the Queen Bee!"

The Waiter lifted its brow. "Is this a *nagger* which I see before me? In that case, forget about it. You are not my employer, and I don't take orders from *you*!" And it swam away to present its drinks to other guests that were waving at it.

"Please, wait!" Alice called after it. "I didn't mean it that way!" But the Waiter ignored her and she was left on her own to devise a plan to meet the Queen.

Before she could come up with another idea, an uproar among the guests interrupted her thoughts. The cause was a large bowl of soup, which was being brought to the table by one of the servants. After it had lifted the lid of the bowl, the soup began rising upwards and spreading throughout the water, which attracted a whole shoal of fish, that kept swimming through with their mouths open in an attempt to eat it. None of them minded where they were going, so they kept slamming into each other. Some even managed to get themselves entangled in the vermicelli, but they were freed soon enough when other fish began nibbling on the threads.

A bit apart from this chaos, there was a section of the garden that seemed to be reserved for the more important guests. To Alice's astonishment, there were a couple of mermaids among them! They were quietly talking to each other, though there was a bit of a disturbance in that part of the garden when one of them found a cichlid happily swimming circles in her wine glass. "Mary!" she cried out to one of her lady's maids in disgust: "This creature is spoiling my drink! Remove it *immediately*!" while the other mermaids were all tut-tutting about how any one *could* have let this happen. But after the fish had been chased off to where it belonged and Mary had replaced her mistress' drink, they rearranged their beautiful long hair and continued chatting as if nothing had happened. It all reminded Alice of a nursery rhyme, which she repeated out loud:—

> *"Mary, Mary, quite contrary,*
> *How does your garden grow?*
> *With silver bells, and cockle shells,*
> *And pretty maids all in a row."*

"Only the silver bells are missing," thought Alice. She had hardly finished the thought, when bells actually began to ring. There was a murmuring among the guests, who all left off what they were doing, and started turning towards the castle. Slowly, the gates opened and then the Queen Bee emerged with her following. Alice made sure she had a place from which she could see everything well, as she now would *finally* get to see what a bee-fish looked like!

Alice first recognised the Trumpeter, who was swimming in front of the Queen to announce her arrival, but then accidentally blocked her way. Confused, he looked to his left and right, appearing to have misplaced her. The Queen Bee made no attempt to hide her annoyance and shoved him aside. Alice noticed that she indeed had the head of a bee—with black and yellow hair, two antennae and huge oval eyes—but her body was that of a flying fish. Next to the Queen Bee there was another important-looking fish, who was wearing a *very* ugly yellow wig. The Haddock noticed Alice looking at him. "That's the King."

"He's no bee either, is he?" inquired Alice.

"No, he is a waspfish," said the Haddock.

"Why is he wearing such a hideous wig? Is he trying to look like a bee?"

"Oh, that's just to make sure he gets noticed. He always feels left out, you see. And over there," the Haddock pointed, "is Prince Dakkar. He's officially royalty, but in fact he's a nobody. You're very lucky to see him at all; he's hardly ever home."

"I thought princes were important," said Alice. "Especially the firstborns. Aren't they supposed to be the heirs?"

"Normally, yes, but the Queen Bee disowned him," said the Haddock. "She has put in her testament that she herself will be the rightful heir to the throne, and all her belongings will go to her, after she dies."

"That does not make sense," said Alice. "How can you inherit the throne after you die?"

"I just told you—she put it in her will," said the Haddock. "And that's a legal document. Are you even listening?"

"She ca'n't become Queen Bee again after she's died, simply because she wo'n't exist anymore!" exclaimed Alice in disbelief.

"Indeed—that's why she'll become Queen Bee II," stated the Haddock matter-of-factly.

"But—" Alice began, but she got interrupted when a school of tetras fluttered past and they had to make way.

"Those are the Queen's new ladyfish," the Haddock continued his explanation. "All staff gets replaced every three days, because of hygiene rules. By the way, all party guests are supposed to have left by then as well, so don't make yourself too comfortable here!"

Indeed the ladyfish that had been surrounding the Queen were now leaving, and the new ladyfish took their places. It was obvious that they did not have a lot of experience, as they seemed to be more in the Queen's way than they were actually helping her. Which did nothing for the Queen's temper. Finally they reached her throne in the garden. It was a giant scallop, opened so one of the shells, which was lined with cushions, formed the seat, and the other shell served as a backrest. A stingray had been secured to the throne with its tail and was swimming above it, making it serve both as a parasol and a fan at the same time. A smaller but similar throne was there for the King, while Prince Dakkar just had to stay afloat. As soon as the Queen and King had taken their seats, two fearsome-looking piranhas positioned themselves in front of them, eyeing any one that dared to come too close, while several others took a place at their sides.

"There goes my plan of just walking up to her," thought Alice sadly.

In the meantime, all kinds of drinks and food were offered to the Queen and King, and the entertainment began. Bright red lobsters showed up and began clapping rhythmically with their claws. They had adorned their bodies with black polkadots—"which makes them look like lady beetles," Alice thought. Some sirens joined in and sang songs with their beautiful voices.

"There must be a way to speak with the Queen," she said to the Haddock and the Red Herring. But they did not seem to hear her—they were both staring at the sirens with their mouths wide open. Alice shoved them.

"What? What?" they shouted, as if coming out of a trance.

"I said: 'There must be a way to speak with the Queen'. Wouldn't you know how to, perhaps?"

"Not me," said the Red Herring, shaking its head. "I'm not important enough."

"You might want to try the butler," said the Haddock, pointing to a black-and-white fish swimming by.

Alice immediately ran after it. "Mister Butler, Sir—" she began, not quite knowing how to address it. The fish turned around, with a questioning look. "I'm sorry to disturb you, you must be awfully busy. But I was hoping you could help me. I'd like to request an audience."

"I think we've got quite one here already," said the Butler, pointing at the guests. "But you'll have to wait until the other performers are done. What are you going to perform? Are you not already on our list?" And it took out a piece of paper, which it began studying after putting on a pair of spectacles.

"I mean, I'd like to make an appointment," Alice tried again.

"And who would you be appointing?" it answered in a stern tone. "There are no vacancies at court, as far as *I* know. Besides, I doubt you have the authority to appoint any one *here.*"

Alice sighed and tried to gather enough patience to rephrase the question again. She decided just to be blunt this time. "The Queen Bee's Scuttleflot is trying to sink my boat. I'd like to make—" But Alice did not get any further. The black-and-white Butler suddenly turned completely pale. "An enemy! There's an enemy of the Queen at court!" it shouted.

This started quite a turmoil. "Get her!" she heard some one screaming, and the piranhas began swimming towards her at high speed.

"Oh dear," thought Alice, "How can I make it clear that I mean no hostilities? Wait, I know! I need a white flag!" And she grabbed the first white thing that she saw—which happened to be the unfortunate Butler. She held the poor thing by its tail and frantically waved it over her head. "Please! I'm here to negotiate!"

The piranhas closed in around her, the Haddock and the Red Herring, but did not attack. Instead, they steered her and the other two towards the Queen Bee's throne.

"And who are *these*?" the Queen Bee asked angrily.

"My name is Alice, your Majesty," said Alice, while making a curtsey.

One of the fish next to the Queen, which was apparently her advisor, moved closer to her and whispered in her ear (but loudly enough that they could overhear it): "I don't know about the child, your majesty, but the other two are convicted felons."

"Am not!" said the Haddock.

"Am too!" said the Red Herring.

There was a confused silence. The Queen was the first to break it. "What crimes are you up to *this* time? Speak!"

"None whatsoever!" exclaimed the Haddock.

"All what-so-never!" exclaimed the Red Herring.

"SILENCE!" bellowed the Queen. "You're making my head hurt!"

"We would never do that, your Majesty. Not to your majestic head," said the Haddock. Alice thought she heard a slight taunting in his voice.

"Much respect there is to bee head," followed the Red Herring with a scarcely hidden grin. "So I bow in front of you."

"But not beehind," added the Haddock. "It would not be civil, this, oh bee-dience." Both could now hardly contain their laughter, which aggravated the Queen even more.

134

"GET THEM OUT OF MY SIGHT!" she roared, after which four piranhas swam forward and drove them away. Which left Alice standing there all by herself. "And now for you," said the Queen. "They tell me you are my enemy. What are you doing here?"

"Pardon me, your Majesty," Alice said politely, "but I am not your enemy. In fact, I have come here to explain just that."

"Then tell me what you have to say in your defence," said the Queen, "but use only one word—let me handle the sentences."

"I'm afraid I cannot explain it in only one word," said Alice.

"There's no need to be afraid, child," said the Queen. "Just obey the rules and you wo'n't be hanged."

To confirm her point, one of the piranhas threateningly pointed to a scaffold next to the castle. There was a fishing line with a hook dangling from it.

"Well?" inquired the Queen. "Answer now. The deadline is getting close!"

"Now," said Alice.

There was silence again. Then the Queen started shouting: "Hang this—" but the King interrupted her just before she could finish her command. "My dear, may I point out to you that she obeyed your order precisely as you requested? Isn't that what you wanted?"

The Queen was obviously not amused, but could not deny that he was right—and that Alice was as well. "All right then," she grumbled. "Let's get on with the charges. You have been marked as my enemy. Do you know how to kill fish?"

Alice thought about this, but could not remember a single time that she had actually killed one. "They are already dead when they are on my plate," she considered, "which means that everything I *think* would kill a fish, would only be a theory, and as long as I don't know for sure, it doesn't count." So eventually she shook her head. As an afterthought she added: "Perhaps Dinah might—"

This remark was not received well. A disturbed mumbling arose from the crowds that had by now gathered around them. "She's a terrorist!" she heard some one exclaim. "Indeed she is!" some one else shouted. That voice sounded familiar, and Alice turned to see who it was. To her surprise, she saw the Tuna floating in the crowds. "She melted my cheese! Came into my study and destroyed my experiments!"

"It melted itself," Alice objected angrily. "You know what *would* have been bad? If I would have *eaten* it afterwards!"

136

The crowds retracted several inches in alarm. There was only one fish that seemingly had been unaware of all that was going on around it, and was left hovering there all by itself. It was the Anglerfish that Alice had met in the cave. Still appearing to be half asleep, she looked up groggily. At length she noticed Alice, smiled feebly, and said: "She's the one who put my light out. I was preparing myself to sleep with the fishies, but then they found me and dragged me to this party." Then she dozed off again.

"That proves it!" the Queen screamed. "You're a terrorist!"

"I'm not a terrorist!" Alice cried out, and pointed at the Queen. "If any one is terrorizing any one, it is *you* and your Scuttleflot!" She could hear the crowds around her gasp and hold their breath. But courageously she continued: "Ever since I fell into this lake—*accidentally* you know—you have been trying to sink my boat!"

"Such impertinence!" shouted the Queen. "To call *me* a terrorist! You can claim it was an accident child, but *I* don't believe a single thing of it! You have come to destroy my imperium, I'm sure of that! But I have caught you in time. You are now *my* subject—and all my subjects must learn to beehive!" she added. "Guards, take her away and put her to work!"

CHAPTER XII

Alice's Objections

TWO piranhas swam towards Alice and chased her along a path that led behind the castle. They ushered her towards a giant beehive, which had been hidden from view when she was in the gardens. "Here, put this on," one of them said, throwing a bundle of clothes towards her. Alice unfolded the bundle. It was a prison uniform, only with black-and-yellow stripes instead of black-and-white ones. As she had no choice but to comply, she obediently put it on as well as she could over her dress. It was obviously not made for humans, but once she had wrestled herself into it, it somehow merged with her own clothes, and she was suddenly wearing a yellow dress with black stripes, and stockings in a similar pattern and colour. As soon as she was dressed, one of the piranhas pressed a large comb into her hands. "Now get to work!" it commanded, while it pushed Alice through the door of the beehive with its snout.

After Alice had entered the beehive, the first thing she did was to take a good look around. The hive was rather crowded, and buzzing with activity. A large number of fish, all dressed in outfits with the same stripes as the one she was wearing, was working on high walls that were made of hexagonal cells, many of them filled to the brim with honey. Most workers were carrying combs like the one she had in her hands, and were busy scraping the walls with them. "Now I finally understand why it's called a honey comb!" thought Alice. "But they ca'n't expect *me* to work here as a punishment? I did not get a fair trial at all!"

When she looked closer, she realised that not all fish were combing. Several of them seemed to have other jobs, mainly to keep the hive clean in general.

138

One fish was busy removing algae from windows. Alice saw another fish using its large tail to sweep the dust on the floors into

little heaps. A third fish was holding a fellow fish by its tail, using it to vacuum up the heaps with its mouth. Behind them followed a fourth fish that was dipping a small squid into a bucket and then used it to mop the floor.

Alice found that the workers were all rather skinny. "Apparently they don't feed them well," Alice concluded. "Are you hungry?" she asked one of the workers when it passed her.

The Worker looked around suspiciously, to make sure nobody saw it talk to Alice. "A little," it confessed. "You see, there is not enough food for all of us workers, there are so many of us here! So we've agreed that we all try to lose weight and get used to eating less. That way, it wo'n't be a problem anymore."

Alice eyed a *very* fat worker fish, who was doing nothing but lie in a corner and munch away on something. "And what about that one? He's not helping and he doesn't look hungry either. Is he not in on the agreement?"

"Oh yes, he is! He is helping to save food as well," said the Worker fish.

"But he is eating way more than the others!"

"Yes, but he is paying for his food, you see. And he is only allowed to buy the food that others haven't eaten because of their diet. It's perfectly fine, because this way, we as a whole are not trying to eat more than there is available for us in total."

"But—that ca'n't be right!" Alice protested.

At that point, the fat fish shouted to Alice: "You have to put your honey where your mouth is, child!"

A much bigger fish swam up to Alice. She assumed it was a supervisor, because it was not dressed in stripes and was carrying a truncheon. The Worker quickly swam away and continued its job. "Start combing!" the Supervisor snarled to Alice.

"I wo'n't," said Alice defiantly. "It's very unfair that I have been sentenced to labour here. I am not guilty of anything, except perhaps not watching my footing very well." Surprised at her own courage, she then dropped the comb, turned around and started running.

"Come back immediately!" the Supervisor called after her. But Alice ran until she had reached the door and emerged outside again. To her great dismay, she found there a line of piranhas waiting for her. The Queen Bee was behind them. Alice came to a halt at once. She looked over her shoulder to see if the Supervisor was chasing her. It had unbuckled its truncheon and was waving it threateningly while it was swimming towards her.

"There's nowhere to run to," said the Queen Bee with an unpleasant grin. "We'll have both you *and* your boat."

"You wo'n't have either of us!" exclaimed Alice frantically. "I wo'n't allow your Scuttleflot to sink our rowing boat. And," turning towards the Supervisor, who had by now reached Alice, "I *wo'n't* let myself get *beaten!*"

To everyone's surprise, a large shell shot up from the lake bottom and disappeared through the surface. The fish around her froze in fear. In the dead silence that followed, the sound of an enormous explosion happening further off in the lake penetrated the court, together with a painful howling.

"*You've SUNK my Scuttleflot!*" the Queen Bee screamed at the top of her voice. "*You savage creature! YOU'VE SUNK IT!*"

At that point, everyone started racing towards Alice: the Supervisor, the piranhas, the Queen, and every other fish that was around. Within seconds she found herself in the middle of a shoal of swarming fish, that almost suffocated her. Their scales felt cold and wet to her skin and she struggled to keep them away from her, but it did not take long before she got completely overwhelmed. "You wo'n't get me!" she kept crying. "You wo'n't get me!" But there seemed to be no stopping them. The fish continued to suffocate her, no matter how hard she tried to shove them away.

"You wo'n't get me! You wo'n't get me!" she repeated. The shoal slowly seemed to become less dense, and instead felt as if the fish were starting to swim up against her in rapid turns. "You wo'n't get me! You wo'n't—"

And then she opened her eyes. She found herself lying on the grass next to the lake shore, in the middle of a rainstorm. Her companions were all frantically trying to repack the food they had distributed on a picnic blanket, to prevent it from getting soaked. The rowing boat was still docked where she remembered leaving it, and it was completely whole.

Alice got up and ran towards them. "Oh, what a curious dream I've had!"

———

Afterwards, back in the boat, she would tell them about all the adventures she had had under water. And that she had decided right there and then, that she would never ever in her life eat a single tilapia fish again. Because, you know, she would always wonder if it could have been the one that had been destined to free Underwaterland from the Queen Bee. The adults would smile and say to her, as they so often had before, what a beautiful mind she had. Her sisters would keep making fun of her because of it, and once they arrived home, her mother would sigh and tell her to stop getting lost in her imagination. But Alice didn't let it bother her at all, because more than any one she knew: not all those who wonder are lost.

THE END.

Look, is that a cameo —
Encrypted in a portmanteau?
We so badly want to know.

Is it mere a pun sublime?
Secrets hidden in the rhyme?
Carroll's meaning's lost in time.

Analysing just a quip;
Ripping pages: censorship!
Reading all as one big trip —

Obviously one gets annoyed;
Leave that scrutiny to Freud;
Literature should be enjoyed!

ABOUT THE AUTHOR

Alice's Adventures under Water is Lenny de Rooy's first book of fiction. Lenny is considered by many to be an expert on the background of Lewis Carroll's *Alice* tales: not only has she studied these books in-dept, and created the website Alice-in-wonderland.net (which she has been maintaining for over 25 years), she also participated in the *Alice in a World of Wonderlands* project, which attempted to inventory all English-language editions and translations of the *Alice* books in the  world. Besides writing and maintaining her website, Lenny loves making music with her two bands, in which she plays the bagpipe and sings, as well as dancing, Live Action Role Playing, re-enactment, dressmaking, and otherwise being creative. In between all her hobbies, Lenny works as an online marketeer at a university. She lives with her cat Sammy in Nijmegen, the Netherlands.

ABOUT THE ILLUSTRATOR

Robert Louis Black has loved drawing since he was a child. During high school he already designed skateboards, T-shirts, and more for friends. Soon he started his own business. In 2012 he completed an associate degree that expanded his skills in other areas of art, like sculpturing, photography, and printmaking. Robert is motivated by all the various assignments he receives from customers, as they challenge him to create something he has never done before. His portfolio currently ranges from tattoo designs to portraits, and from shop window paintings to murals. And now he can also add illustrating a book to the list! Robert lives with his son Christopher in Manhattan Beach, United States. In his spare time he enjoys running, basketball, playing the piano and guitar, reading, and skateboarding.

You can find more of his work on www.robertlouisblack.com.

www.ingramcontent.com/pod-product-compliance
Lightning Source LLC
La Vergne TN
LVHW051537170726
843492LV00006B/1815